October Falls

October Falls

Judith Erickson

Independent Publisher

Taylors Falls, Minnesota

Contents

Author's Note

This book has been a long-time in coming to this point. Begun as a young professional, the work became interrupted when my professional career took off. Add in marriage, family, launching and being part of a family business all took priority and time. I did work on parts in and around these seasons and now with the pandemic of 2020, I determined to use this opportunity to finally launch October Falls into the world!

Prelude

Searching and
dreaming of love
is such a waste of time
For when the time is right
love will come.

The mountain was not difficult to climb, if you knew what you were doing. The trail wound through rocky terrain and in many places it is difficult to see and follow. Above the tree line across rough rocky slopes rock cairns marked the route to the ridge-top summit route. There the trail was marked by the old Forest Service telephone poles which lead to the summit. The summit was marked by a pile of boulders known as the fort, the site of a Forest Service lookout station, long ago abandoned.

The view was a disappointment. Although Mt. McLoughlin was the highest peak in southern Oregon, the clouds that had surrounded her all day filled in the valleys and prevented her from seeing Three Sisters or Mt. Shasta.

A gusty wind blew around the rocks, bringing a shiver from her even as it chilled the sweat on her brow. It was an invigorating climb, her heart pounded loudly in her chest as she surveyed the area, hands on hips, legs slightly apart, braced against the wind that was turning her sweat to trickles of ice.

She turned, pushing a hand absently through her blond tangled hair, and went inside what remained of the four rocky walls of the fort. It was empty except for the wind that came howling through the cracks. Pulling off her day pack she sat, leaning against one of the largest boulders. Inside her pack she had lunch and a book. Another shiver ran through her and she pulled her coat closer, pulling the collar tightly around her neck. With fingers of ice she took her lunch out and began to eat.

A shout went up behind her. Then she heard a different one. She smiled even as she shivered. John and Jason had found the chimney rock. But the smile was quickly replaced with a frown of concern. They didn't have any ropes and climbing the chimney rock without them was dangerous. She stuffed her sandwich back into her pack and hurried out of the fort. She bent her head into the wind as she made her way to where the mountain fell away.

Voices echoed up through a crack in the mass of stone piled against the mountain's edge. Carefully she lowered herself over the edge of the chimney. The wind blasted up. Whistling and moaning amongst the rock it shot through her coat into her bones.

Scrambling she climbed back into the open, breathless. She stood there, troubled and indecisive as the wind continued to buffet her, daring her to tempt fate, spread her arms and fly with the clouds.

She turned in a circle to study the ominous grumbling clouds closing in. Letting out a sigh she sat. Her grey eyes softened and a smile played on her lips as she longed for a warm fire.

The wind continued its cold penetration and her shivers became uncontrollable. She pulled her knees in and hunched her shoulders, bringing the collar of her coat to the tips of her numb ears. Her blond hair blew in wisps around her face as she tried to go deeper into her coat.

She closed her eyes, memorizing the feeling of being high in the mountains. In her mind she could see the mountains very clearly. Their awe-inspiring peaks. The clouds that made patterns and shadows on the green slopes. The golden aspen reflected in the still mountain lakes. The clear tumbling streams. The white of the glaciers as they glistened in the sun. She would miss this.

"Hey."

She opened her eyes. John was crawling over the top of the chimney.

"What are you doing here?"

She couldn't help but smile at his enthusiasm and surprise. "I couldn't study anymore. This is our last day out and I wanted to be with you guys up here. So I put my books away and here I am."

He peered closer. "Are you okay?"

"I'm cold."

"Cold's not the word, you're almost blue."

She shrugged and made a concentrated effort not to shiver.

"How long have you been here?"

"Since you and Jason went down the chimney."

"That's been quite a while."

"Where's Jason?"

"Here." Jason came over the edge to stand by John.

"Don't you guys know that is dangerous? I've been sitting here worried."

"And freezing to death," continued John. "You're turning blue. You need to go down. Now. You, of all people should know the risks and the symptoms of hypothermia!" He reached down and pulled her up roughly.

"I guess you're right." She leaned against him as another gust of wind blew up through the tunnel.

"There's no question. We are going to go. Now." He began to walk toward the fort, pulling her along.

"No." She stopped, pulling her arm free. "You don't need to babysit me. I can get back fine by myself. I'll wait for you at the trail head."

"I don't think so."

"I do. I've been here before. I know this mountain. I know you want to explore more, you guys stay and enjoy it a while, then come down. I'll be fine as soon as I get out of this wind."

John opened his mouth to protest but she held up her hand to cut him off, her grey eyes hardening in determination.

"Okay." John held up his hands in surrender. The sooner he quit arguing with her, the sooner she would leave. They would wait a few minutes and then follow. He didn't think she was in as good of shape as she wanted them to believe.

"Be careful." She looked meaningfully at each in turn before smiling. "See you soon." She turned and in moments they could see her making her way along the ridge line. Then she disappeared.

Chapter One

My sleeping mind
stirs to note
That it is fall.
The air is cool.
The sleep is deep
my lips part
in a sigh at
some blissful dream
as my dead limbs
snuggle deeper
under the quilts
while my mind
stirs to note
That it is fall.
The air is cool.

She could feel the wind flying through her hair, touching her ears before swirling down around her neck. She pulled her coat closer and tried to get her ears under the collar. It didn't work. The cold penetrated deeper and deeper. She felt numb, her legs were like lead and her ankles threatened to give way with every step she took. The terrain was rough and rocky, but she didn't slow. Ahead the tree line was coming into sight as she rounded the last outcropping of rock before the trail went below the tree line.

She thought only of the warm fire waiting. Its flames were leaping into the night, dancing the cold away. She could see into its deep blue depths. Its smoldering embers snapped and crackled, sending sparks flying out beyond the circle of light, high into the night, to the stars. It was warm, oh so warm. She reached out her hands . . .

A film of sweat broke out on her forehead. She pushed at the heavy covers, reaching out her hands she woke when they touched a warm body instead of rough cold stone. Her eyes flew open as two arms came around her and held her tight.

The nightmare left her as she realized she was lying against a man. She could feel his hand in her hair.

"Shh...It's okay." He was saying softly into her ear. He pulled his head back. Although this wasn't her first nightmare, it was the first time she'd awakened.

Her fevered eyes met his and she found herself caught in their brown depths. The confusion left her as she reached out to touch him. As she did, sleep overtook her and she drifted off, her hand still on his cheek.

Chase Harrington stared thoughtfully into the night

remembering how he had found her, unconscious and cold, at the bottom of the gully. He had been high on the mountain to a place where the rock gave way, opening into a grassy basin with a clear lake at its base. Lodgepole pine clustered along its edge, except at the far side where granite bluffs closed the basin. It was a cold, windy day. He was thankful he had once taken the time to build a small shelter. It was a place he came to when he hit a wall writing and needed to clear his head.

As the long shadows of dusk began to fill the basin, Chase poured water on the fire. After stirring the charred remains he picked up the book of poems he had been reading and stepped out into the open. A raw north wind swirled through the basin and he pulled his jacket tighter about him. He called for his dog, Jake, and they began the hike back to his cabin.

He stayed longer than planned and the long shadows urged him to hurry. A mile remained when he noticed Jake was gone. He began to retrace his steps. He stopped and listened.

"Jake!" He called.

He heard the dog barking off to his right. He went toward the sound, off the trail through a dense tangle of brush to the edge of a deep gully. The sun had set and the light was almost gone. In the dim shadows he picked his way down the rough rock-strewn side and as he reached its narrow bottom he heard Jake's voice more strongly and clearly. When he finally saw his black lab he whistled to him impatiently. The dog ran to him, but as Chase turned to leave, Jake stopped and returned to the spot where he had been. With the onslaught of darkness Chase was anxious to get to the cabin. He called to Jake again. This time Jake refused to leave. Finally, Chase went to him.

He was not prepared for what he found. He knelt down and gently turned over the body slumped against an old stump. He found himself starring into the ashen face of a young woman. He reached for her wrist. Her skin was like ice and her lips were blue, unbelievably blue. Her pulse was weak but she was alive. He knew he needed to act quickly. He didn't have a lot of options.

He wrapped her in his jacket and lifted her into his arms. Moving as gently as he could over the rough terrain in the dark he was relieved to finally reach the cabin. Flinging back the covers he laid her in the middle of the bed covering her while he got another heavy wool blanket. He gently removed her clothing down to a t-shirt and underwear. He quickly removed his own clothes and slipped into bed. Pulling her to him he had held her, warming her body with his. There were simply no other options. He had to get her warm, then he would deal with what came next.

He spoke softly into her ear and gradually the shivering left and she slept peacefully until the fever came. He watched over her all that first night and sat at her side during the day, trying to keep ice on her right foot and elevated.

Now in the pale moonlight Chase studied the sleeping woman he held in his arms. A light film of sweat covered her and her breathing was ragged. She stirred against him when he touched the dark swell just above her right eye.

She had given him a scare, he thought, as he eased away. As far as he could tell she didn't have any broken bones, but she was cut and bruised and her right ankle was twice its normal size. She had tumbled quite a distance before meeting up with that old stump. She was lucky she was alive, lucky he had found her.

He wondered what lay behind that battered exterior. He had gone through her backpack and only learned the barest of details. Given the weather outside, he would have time to learn more. He closed his eyes, and resting his cheek against her soft hair he slept, deeply and contently, at peace with himself and, for once, with the world.

#

Reaching out Katherine Carlson moved to where the warmth had been. Gone. She lay, letting consciousness come back slowly. She had been in a deep sleep and her dreams left her confused. She remembered a man with dark brown eyes who held her tight. She opened her eyes and struggled to sit up. The movement sent a sharp jab of pain through her and she groaned.

She lay where she fell, hurting everywhere. Pulling in a deep breath she tried to clear her head and think. Where was she? What had happened?

Using her left foot, it didn't hurt like her right one, she kicked the covers partially off then curled up around them. Her head hurt, her whole body ached, and her right ankle throbbed. With fevered eyes she stared across the bed at an oak chest of drawers. A frown marred her forehead. It was so quiet. Where was she?

She remembered the brown eyes of her dream. Her grey eyes softened as she remembered how strangely warm and secure she had felt in his arms.

It was just a dream. She pushed her hair off her face and sighed. She hugged the covers to her and closed her eyes feeling overwhelmed. She slept.

Sputtering and coughing Katie woke up to find herself face to face with her dream.

"You." She said and stared. Her eyes moved slowly taking in his dark stubble and long perfect nose, to his lips which held a hint of a smile before meeting his eyes which held a mixture of surprise and pleasure. He had never before seen eyes like hers; they were the color of a late winter sky, slate grey, clear and deep.

"You're real." She whispered. Then, becoming aware he was sitting beside her, his arm across her back holding her against him, she stiffened. "What's going on?"

He studied her a moment longer, before he took his arm away, and stood. "Here." He said, handing her a steaming mug. "Drink this."

"What is it?" She asked, confused.

"Just chicken broth."

"It smells horrible."

"Drink it." He said again and straddled a chair she hadn't seen near the bed. She took a tentative sip and saw his small smile as she made a face at the taste. A smile that turned to concern when she winced and touched the dark bruise on her temple. He met her questioning, bewildered look.

"Listen." Chase said and came around to sit beside her, absently brushing her bangs out of her eyes. He smiled slowly and she watched, amazed.

"You're pretty banged up and you've been sick. This bruise," he reached out and touched it, "will soon be gone." He smiled again and stood. "Now you have to drink this broth if you expect to get better."

She watched him intently, her eyes never leaving his. Her head felt heavy and she didn't really hear him. She only saw the tender concern in his eyes and was disturbed that she felt so comfortable with a stranger.

"How long?" She asked.

He stopped. "What?"

"How long before I'm better."

"I don't know, only you do."

"Right." She didn't press the matter but drank the thick spicy broth to the last drop.

"Good." He took the mug from her. "Now go back to sleep."

She shrugged and watched him sit in the chair near her and before drawing in a deep breath and closing her eyes.

Katie slept the restless troubled sleep of the sick. She was at first hot and kicked off the covers. Then she was cold and couldn't get warm. When Chase woke her she obediently took the mug from his hand and drank its contents. As soon as he took it from her she fell back asleep. He stayed with her through the second day, wiping the sweat away when she was burning and holding her in her nightmares. After dark sometime, the fever broke.

Late, in the night when Katie felt him next to her she woke. Moonlight streamed through the window. The night was clear and bright. She reached out a hand to touch him, but caught herself. She didn't want to wake him. And, if he were a dream, she didn't want him to disappear. Instead she studied his face, memorizing its lines to take with her when she left.

Suddenly his eyes were open. Silently he looked at her as if she were the dream. When his arms came around her, she didn't resist. He brushed his lips lightly against hers. "Go back to sleep," he said as he eased her to his side. "We'll talk in the morning."

Katie closed her eyes but didn't sleep. She could still feel the light touch of his lips. She felt the slow even beat of his heart and wondered in whose arms she was sleeping.

Two

When Katie woke he was gone. A shaft of sunlight fell across the bed. She stretched. It hurt. She opened her eyes. Her body ached but she felt better. She lifted her arms above her and stretched again trying to ease the stiffness out of her limbs. It hurt.

She sat up and looked around her. She was in the L of an L shaped room. On one side were the oak chest and the abandoned chair near the bed. His, she thought.

She turned her attention to the window. From her position she couldn't see what was outside. Was she still in the mountains?

Sighing she ran her hand absently through her hair. Where was she? It was then she realized she was clad only in a flannel shirt. Who undressed her?

Footsteps sounded and as she raised her eyes she knew.

"Feeling better?" Chase asked as he sat in the chair.

"Yes." Her grey eyes were wary and she made a point of pulling the blankets up. She glanced out the window. "What time is it?"

"Around noon."

"Oh." She studied her hands searching her mind for something to say. Who was he? Then she remembered the night. Her eyes swept the room nervously before she could meet his gaze. She tried a small smile. "Thank you for helping me." She paused, her grey eyes perplexed. "How long have I been here?"

"Over two days."

"Does anyone know where I am?"

He hesitated before answering. "No. You were pretty far from any trail. Were you lost?"

"I don't remember."

"Were you with anyone?"

"Not at the time." Katie felt sick. No one knew where she was, that she was alive and well. They were to have arrived home yesterday. Two days and no word from her.

She leaned forward. "Can you get in touch with my family? They must be sick from worry. Tell them I'll be home in a couple of days. Have them call school. Stan can take my place until I get there." She spoke rapidly, thinking aloud.

Chase held up his hands. "Hold on, one thing at a time. We'll go as soon as we can."

At her questioning look he said, "I don't have a phone. This cabin is pretty remote. If it has rained, I can't get out. It rained yesterday. I think we can get out tomorrow, if the weather holds." He paused, concern filling his dark eyes. "I'm sure they've sent out search and rescue teams. I wish there was a way to get in touch with them, but I didn't want to leave you alone. So, if we can, I'd like to take care of that and take you to the hospital and get you checked out. You took a nasty fall. I don't think you have any major injuries, and I don't think anything is broken, but you've been out cold. I found you two nights ago slumped against a tree stump at the bottom of a rough rocky gulley."

"So that's what happened." Katie mumbled.

"You don't remember?"

"No." She said softly.

"Can you touch your nose with your right hand?" He asked.

She looked at him strangely and did as he asked.

"All right, that's good." He said. "You've been unconscious the better part of two days. I just need to do this to see. If we were in Medford, this is what they would do at the hospital. Now, take your left hand, raise your right index finger and move it slowly in front of your face. Can you follow it from left to right and back again?"

Again, she did as he asked.

"That's good, okay."

Suddenly she was tired. She slumped back against the pillows. She was so confused. She hadn't planned for this. She was supposed to be back in Minnesota, teaching history to college kids, not lying half naked in a strange man's bed, broken and weak.

Her eyes clouded, tears threatened to spill over. Then he was there. His arm came around her pulling her close to him. His hand was in her hair. "Don't worry." He said. "It'll all work out." She felt his lips on her forehead.

She met his eyes and was startled by what she saw. The tears were held in check. "Yeah. I guess so. I . . ." She broke off, uncertain. "I just didn't plan for this."

"Neither did I."

Of course, he hadn't. She managed a small smile. He hesitated a minute, wanting to hold her longer. But he stood and stepped away. "You rest now. I'll get you something to eat."

"Not broth."

"Not broth."

"Good." She snuggled back into the pillows. Who was he? She watched him leave the room. Why did he seem so familiar? Why did she feel so safe with a stranger?

As he left, he paused in the doorway, "Is there anyone besides your family who would be concerned?"

"No. Well, yes, my friends."

He was surprised to be relieved by her answer. Her presence and the need to tend to her injuries and her had interrupted his summer work, but strangely he didn't resent it. That didn't mean he was going to spend a lot of time thinking about it, or her. As soon as he could, he would take her into town, get her checked out at the local hospital and send her home. There would be time to get back on schedule to meet his fall deadline.

While she waited for him to return, Katie studied the part of the room in which she lay and beyond. The more she saw the more uncomfortable she became and felt like she was intruding on his privacy.

He had antiques, very old and carefully restored. The quilts on the bed were homemade. The floors were of beautiful hardwoods, covered in areas with large braided rugs of muted colors. There was a fireplace on the far side of the room, sharing a wall with floor to ceiling built-in shelves filled with books. She wished she could read their titles, it would tell her more.

A dark leather couch was placed in the center of the room in front of the fireplace. There was a door which she presumed led outside. A window like the one in her portion of the room shed light onto a small table covered, as near as she could tell, with photographs.

It was all very neat, comfortable, warm and inviting. Everything, it seemed, except her, had its own perfect place in the system of things. She had disrupted the order of his life, the peace of his home.

She closed her eyes, pondering her situation. She had to leave. How soon? She felt so weak, so tired. She remembered his words, as soon as the weather permitted, he would help her. She didn't like being out of control.

She thought of him. She could feel his arms around her, could see the tenderness in his eyes. She wanted to feel his lips touch hers again.

No. Her eyes flew open. What was she thinking of? She didn't even know his name.

She sat up and concentrated on smoothing out the bed covers as she sought to calm her chaotic racing thoughts. Why did she feel so at peace here? Why did she feel a sense of security when he held her?

Because, she reasoned, her eyes sweeping the cabin once again, the cabin was a peaceful place, in the mountains. And she was not her normal self. He was a good man who had done what needed to be done, nothing more. He did what was necessary to save her life. She felt secure in his arms because he saved her life. Because of him, she was alive. She would be eternally grateful, but that was it.

She would be able to resume her life as planned, a little behind schedule, but she'd make it work. It never occurred to her to question why he held her or why he kissed her.

When Chase returned she was composed, in control, her confidence restored. She was disheveled, a dark bruise marred her clear skin, yet there was a certain sense of purpose in the way she held her head. Her eyes held a new light of determination. Only a trace of his smile remained when he set a heavy tray before her.

"Thank you." Her gaze wavered momentarily when her eyes met his. She gave the food her full attention. A fat fluffy omelet stuffed with veggies and cheese, toast, and milk. No broth.

Chase didn't miss the change. He was surprised to note a feeling of disappointment as he recognized the determination in her grey eyes. They challenged him, taunted him to care. Just try it, he read, I don't need anyone. But then he remembered her last night, eyes wide and wondering, vulnerable. There was something there, but now was not the time to dwell on it.

"I'll just have to take things in stride." He muttered to himself.

"What?" She looked up.

He paused to study her face. His scrutiny unnerved her and she resumed eating.

"I said it was probably time for introductions."

He had her attention.

"Chase Harrington."

She stared, determination forgotten. "Chase Harrington?" She whispered.

"Is something wrong?" His eyes narrowed and he leaned forward.

"Oh, no. I . . ." She trailed off. "I never expected you to look like. . ." She tried again. "I don't know what I expected, certainly not you."

Color rapidly claimed her cheeks.

"I see." He sat back, and even though he already knew, he asked, "And who are you? Do you remember your name?"

"Katherine Carlson, Katie."

There was a scratching noise at the door. "Excuse me." Chase left as Katie tried to restore the calm confidence which had been so quickly lost only moments before. She took a deep breath as if more air would slow her racing heart.

Who would have thought? Chase Harrington here? She had read all his books. She taught one of them in her contemporary affairs class each fall. It was her favorite book of her favorite class.

But it was more than that she taught one of his books, much more.

When she felt herself being swallowed by her schedule, when she needed to be reminded of why she taught what she taught, she would read Harrington.

It was his sense of caring, his deep commitment to care and nurture others and the earth in which he lived that first drew her to him. He believed in the common good. His arguments for unselfish living and stewardship of time, resources and relationships stood in stark contrast to the rugged American individualism that wrestled its way to achievement.

Harrington's was a clear voice amidst chaos and greed. It held the peace and serenity of clear mountain air, not the polluted thought of one who had lost touch with the earth and its fullness. He could take complex issues of the day, offer a clear analysis and present choices and consequences. You were required to think if you read his books. He didn't spoon feed you.

Harrington seemed content with his life, but spoke against the consumerism and greed that was consuming the world at a rapid pace, leaving in its wake a world impoverished in natural and human resources. As the rich in the world were getting richer, the poor were getting poorer, and the middle stayed locked in mediocrity. He wrote of alternatives;

of looking at the trees in the forest; the foothills of the mountains and the drop of rain in a lake.

Katie was intimate with his ideas and felt certain camaraderie with his thought. Often, she found herself arguing his points to others, only to be shunted aside as an idealist.

She had always wondered what he was like in person. Now, she knew. Now she knew why she felt so safe in his arms, so secure with a stranger. He was no stranger. She had known him a long, long time. She had always assumed he was a much older man, but she was wrong, so wrong.

3

Three

Her eyes never left him as he went to the door and opened it briefly. When he turned around brown eyes met grey. Her eyes were troubled and she wore an unbearably serious expression on her face. The confidence was gone from the lift of her chin because she no longer had the strength to maintain it. Yet there was a glimmer of hope behind the clouds; a sense of breathless anticipation.

His eyes never left hers and as he neared the bed she could see into their warm brown depths. She thought she was going to drown in them. Then suddenly they were twinkling and a half smile stole his lips.

"Katherine, Katie Carlson," he said formally, liking the sound of her name. "I'd like you to meet Jake."

He watched her closely as she noticed Jake for the first time. He was a large black lab with a harmless look, his dark eyes full of affection.

"Hello Jake." She said and reached out to pat his head.

Chase heard the weariness in her voice.

"Come on Jake." He said. "Go lay down. You can see Katie tomorrow."

Katie, huh, she thought. It was pretty easy for him to slip into the familiarity that only a few people used. The defiance came back. He read it quickly and decided she needed to go to sleep. He picked up the tray of half eaten food to follow Jake. Was she not hungry or did something cause her to lose her appetite?

He stopped.

"Did you get enough to eat?" He asked.

"Yes." She whispered suddenly feeling alone. "I couldn't eat any more. I wanted too, but I just couldn't. I'm so tired." She crawled down into the quilts. But as he began to turn away she said. "Wait."

He turned back again.

"Are we going to try to leave tomorrow?"

"Yes." He said. "We'll try."

"Try? I'm really worried about no one knowing where I am."

He came back to her bedside. "I know I don't like it either. But I can't do anything about it. Go to sleep. Okay." He bent down and kissed her lightly on the cheek. "Get some sleep, tomorrow could be a busy day." He said softly.

She simply nodded and closed her eyes.

While Katie slept Chase worked. He was beginning to feel the pressure of falling behind the deadlines he had set for himself. The hour grew late as he valiantly tried to regain his discipline and organize his thoughts. He read and made notes to himself but he couldn't concentrate, his mind kept returning to the woman sleeping in his bed. Again, and again he found himself trying to understand her startled reaction to him when she found out his name. He fought to keep a tight rein on his thoughts and concentrate on his reading.

Finally, he threw down his pencil and gave up trying. There would be time to catch up when she was better and gone. His solitude and focus had been turned upside down. He flipped off the light sending the cabin into darkness except for the faint glow of the dying fire. By its meager light he quietly watched the shadows flicker across her sleeping form. For a long while he stood there, absorbed, fighting over her with himself, longing to take her in his arms to hold her there forever. Knowing that keeping her would be next to impossible, he whispered her name and left.

#

She felt seasick. Her stomach fell to her feet. Looking out across the panoramic view she felt weakened by the heights. She sat down a safe distance from the edge and contemplated the scene below. Gradually the eerie sickness passed. She felt someone come beside her. She didn't know his name or who he was. He was darkly handsome, in a rough strong way. He was dressed in jeans, a soft flannel shirt of red and blue tones and held a rag sweater in his hand. He smiled at her as he sat down. They began to talk, first about the view, then about themselves. She felt warmth begin to spread through her blood. They stopped talking, brown eyes held grey and she had the feeling that she had waited a long time for him to come into her life. She felt alive, wondrously alive. Suddenly, without warning she was flying in space and the earth came rushing up to meet her. As the darkness crushed her, she heard him laughing, laughing, and laughing.

Katie woke with a sharp gasp. Startled out of a deep sleep she tried to shake the dread of impending doom. Pale morning light filtered through the window. Sleep pulled at her but she chased it off, preferring the uncertain realities of the day to the disturbing dreams of night.

She felt the bed sag beside her and looked into the eyes of her dream. A soft sigh of relief escaped her when he pulled her against him.

"Chase?" She asked tentatively.

"Hmm. It's all right now." He spoke softly as he lightly stroked her back, losing his fingers in her hair.

"You're real?" Again, the tentative question, "Not a dream?"

"I'm real." He held her off so he could look into her grey eyes clouded with uncertainty and sleep.

The seriousness of his dark eyes caught at her. No! I'm only deceiving myself, she thought frantically as his lipsclaimed hers in a tender kiss. It wasn't something he had planned, but when he felt her resistance turn, the kiss turned into something more, even though he knew there could be no more.

Katie felt something shift inside her as she gave herself up to the kiss. Through sheer determination he broke the kiss, but didn't pull away. They held each other close. It was a long moment, each lost in the turmoil of their own emotions as they tried to restore reason to its proper role. Only the soft sound of the fire burning disturbed the silence. Katie was scared to her toes.

Finally, she spoke. "I'd like to get up. I'd like to, leave, if we can."

He moved away and stood, but their eyes held. I dare you, hers challenged. I dare you to care.

He turned away reaching for a bundle of clothes by the chest. He threw the clothes to her. "Here, they're clean. If you'd like to take a shower, the bathroom is through that door."

"Thank you." She clutched the clothes tightly as he retreated from the determined gleam in her eyes.

She got up from the bed and was immediately dizzy. She sat down abruptly. With a tight shake of her head the feeling passed. Taking a deep breath, she tried again. She stood slowly, anticipating the disconcerted loss of balance. It didn't come. Relieved, she took a tentative step forward. A shower would feel so good, she felt so grimy and dirty, her hair in tangles. She was embarrassed as she remembered him touching her hair. Ugh.

Later when she was clean, she put on her own clothes, glad to be out of his flannel shirt. She clutched it to her a moment, then set it aside. She felt ready to face the rest of the day.

#

Chase was nowhere in sight. But everything in the room

gave evidence of his presence. There was no doubt this was Chase Harrington's home.

She stood, feeling lost and uncertain of herself. She fought the urge to fly to the bed and bury herself under the quilts and seek the serenity of sleep.

Instead she took in his desk, which dominated the remainder of the living area. Papers and books were stacked about. His computer was silent. This cabin not only was where he lived but where he came to work, to write.

Where was this cabin? She frowned, perplexed that she didn't know where she was or how she got here. She would ask him.

Suddenly she felt his presence in the room. Turning too quickly she lost her balance and found herself in his arms. He held her loosely, his face void of all expression.

"I see you've made it up." Chase said.

"Barely," she hesitated. Then a smile warmed her eyes.

She moved out of his arms to the front window. "It's snowing." She leaned on the windowsill in dismay, mesmerized by the swirling, churning snow. She could feel the strength of the wind through the glass. Her nose was cold.

"Yeah, it started last night."

"Isn't it early? How long will it last?" She asked anxiously over her shoulder.

He shrugged indifferently. "I don't know. I don't think it will last long. In the mountains, you never know."

"I know."

He stood at his desk, sorting through his notes. "I've got

work I need to do. Make yourself at home. We're not going to be able to leave today."

Katie was gripped with a sense of hopeless desperation. No one knew where she was, she didn't know where she was and wasn't in control of her emotions. The minute she got a grip on herself, he shattered it with a smile or a touch. What was happening? She clasped her arms together across her chest and followed the dance of the descending snow. A tear blinded her vision and she hastily wiped it away. What was the matter with her? She never cried.

Chase looked up in time to see her wipe at her eyes. "I'm sorry." He said.

She turned from the window, eyes once again dry. "It's not your fault." She forced a weak smile. "I'm hungry. Where is the kitchen?" She looked for a door.

He pushed away from the desk. "Let me get something for you."

"No." She said. She needed to put some distance between them. "I can do it. You've done enough for me already. Where's Jake?"

"He's in the kitchen." Chase pointed to the swinging door. "Eggs, bread, milk, cheese, and fruit is in the fridge. Pans are next to the stove. Everything else is above the stove. If you need anything let me know." He returned his attention to his work.

The snow beat relentlessly against the large bay window which dominated the kitchen. The flakes settled on the trees only to be shaken loose with every renewed gust of wind.

Their boughs scraped roughly against the back of the cabin. Despite the fierceness of the storm, it was a warm place. Jake was snuggled in his corner inside the door. He greeted Katie with a lift of the head and he seemed to smile before settling back to sleep.

She found everything just where Chase said she would. She was amazed at the neatness and order. While the coffee brewed she made eggs and toast.

As she sat at the table in front of the bay window, her thoughts were far beyond the snow storm raging beyond the protective panes of glass. She remembered the first time she had climbed this mountain, back when she was in college. She spent the fall semester of her Junior year in an extension program located in an old logging camp in southern Oregon. Her hiking boots didn't arrive until mid-September so she climbed in tennis shoes and quickly came to appreciate the consequences of being unprepared in the mountains.

That fall was among the best times of her life. They lived an isolated, quiet community. She met the intellectual, spiritual and physical challenges of the program head on. She learned not only academically, but personally and grew as only young twenty-somethings do. Her outlook on life changed forever.

Their mountain living was simple and unpretentious. The shared community meant meal preparation and eating were done together. This lent to conversations and friendships that she still counted amongst the best of her life. Even in graduate school there had never been such a blending of ideas or a desire on her part to wrestle with huge questions. She remained disciplined but didn't have the drive she had that fall. There were too many distractions outside of the mountains.

That was why they had come west. They decided to follow the 1804 route of Lewis and Clark, over the northern plains to Oregon. They took two weeks to follow the route west. Then they took time to explore Oregon. They attended the Shakespeare Theater in Ashland, had gone white water river rafting on the Rouge River and finally they had come to the Sky Lakes Wilderness to camp and hike.

They came here to clear the garbage from their brains, to touch the real, and for Katie, to find once again the peace the mountains held.

With each passing mile westward, she felt the tension begin to lift. They had decided not to buy any papers or listen to the radio. They didn't want to know what was going on, they wanted a break from breaking news. The wide-open skies spread before them, drawing them on to the majestic strength of the mountains. By the time she sat huddled and cold at the top of the mountain her spirit was renewed. She felt ready to go back.

Now that was changed. She didn't know where or how she lost her way, how she came to be at the bottom of a gully, or how Chase Harrington came to find her. But everything was changed, everything.

Absently she lifted her mug to her lips. Cold! Ugh! She stood to refresh her coffee but her legs didn't hold her as a wave of dizziness claimed her sense of balance. She fell with a clatter.

Jake barked and came to her.

Chase burst into the room as Katie began to pick herself up. He reached down to help her. As she came unsteadily to her feet she gave a tight shake of her head and put a hand to the dark bruise at her temple.

"What happened?" He asked her brusquely, totally unaware that his fingers were digging painfully into her shoulders.

Her raised eyes met his and she was disconcerted by what she saw there. Normally she could handle these situations. But she was out of her depth here. She didn't understand her own feelings, the strength of the attraction, much less trying to figure out his. Her initial uncertainty was replaced with her battered determination.

"I-I stood up too fast and got dizzy." She said, grey eyes still interlocked with brown. As his eyes softened she almost breathed a sigh of relief. Instead she said, "I'm okay. I've just got to remember to move more slowly."

He saw her relief and determination. The light went out of his eyes and he released her. Looking at the shattered mug on the floor he said, "I'll clean this up. You go in the other room and rest."

Katie stared at the broken pieces, her thoughts as fragmented as the mug. "I'm sorry." She said in a small voice. She watched Chase get the broom from behind the refrigerator. "Umm. . ."

"Yes?" He stopped.

"Can I have another cup of coffee?"

He frowned momentarily. "Yes. But I'll bring it to you when I'm finished. Now go and rest."

Katie fled as quickly as her bad ankle would allow her. Chase began to sweep up the floor. He caught Jake watching him. He stopped.

"Don't look at me like that." He said.

"What was I supposed to do?" He asked. Kneeling he patted him on the head.

"Right," he looked into Jake's amber eyes.

"You're supposed to be my friend."

The dog didn't even blink.

"You think you know so much, Jake." He looked at the closed door.

"Why don't you go and keep her company?" He stood and resumed his task. Jake didn't move.

"Go on." He said. "Get out of here. Leave me alone for a while, okay?"

Jake hesitated but complied quickly when Chase shot him a stern look and pointed a finger to the door.

Katie was going to drive him mad. He needed to figure out how get past the snow, get her into town, checked out and connect her with her family and friends. Maybe he could leave her here, find someone with search and rescue. They had to be looking, he reasoned. He could bring them here and they could take it from there. He simply did not know, with the snow, how he could get her out himself. He would go with her, of course, make sure she was okay. But then he could get back to his quiet, normal life.

4

Four

The crackling orange tipped flames of the fire drew Katie to the fireplace. She stood, absorbed, without seeing, trying to comprehend what had passed between them in the kitchen. She failed.

Jake came to her then and she sat, draping her arms around him, holding him close to her. Her head was filled with Chase's intense dark brown eyes. She could still feel where his hands had gripped her shoulders.

She sighed and ran a hand through her hair. "What do you think, Jake?" She asked, releasing him. His amber eyes seemed sad and she had the uncanny feeling he knew something she didn't.

"Silly dog," she said and playfully pushed him away.

"Yes, he is sometimes. But he saved your life."

At the sound of his voice, Katie jumped.

"Here's your coffee." Chase handed her a mug.

"Thank you." She said.

Their eyes held for a few more moments before she turned away. Resting her head on her knees she once again contemplated the dancing flames of the fire. She heard papers rustle and knew Chase was at his desk, working.

She felt the loneliness and worry begin to creep in. The self-pity returned. She was injured and stranded in a strange place, with a strange man, with nothing to do but watch the fire and think about…about whatever. School? No, it was no good. They would be getting ready to start by now. What would happen to her classes? Would they eliminate them? Or would Stan take over?

John and Jason, where were they? Home? Here?

Mom and Dad must be sick, with worry.

No. She took a tentative sip of the coffee. No, there was no point sitting there worrying about things she had no control over. There would be plenty of time for that later, when she finally got home.

What then? She supposed it was just as well that he worked and ignored her. She was at a complete loss to explain how she felt about him. And she didn't want to think about that either. That too, would sort itself out later, when she was home.

What to do then, to keep the loneliness and worry from creeping into the corners of her mind, to keep her from thinking about being here, with him. Books. He had books.

Her mood brightened marginally. She went to the shelves. All the books she expected him to have were there and more.

With pleasure she ran a knowing eye across their titles. She stopped, startled.

Uneasiness began to creep into her stomach. She reached up and pulled down a slim volume. It was a collection of her poetry. The cover was worn. She opened it. Chase Harrington's name is scrawled along the top of the title page. It is his book.

As she read through it she realizes why it is in such bad shape. Passages are underlined. There was writing in the margin. He had read and analyzed it, she can see it in the notes. She collected herself and carefully put it back where she found it. It was written in her pen name. He wouldn't know. He couldn't. Just the thought of him knowing she was the author was frightening. She was confused enough as it was.

The pleasure was gone. Yet she continued to look for something to take her mind off her situation. He had a substantial number of novels; surely, she could find something to read. She found a classic western novel and settled on the couch. Reading for her was effortless, but today she found it hard to concentrate. Often her mind strayed to the man who seemed oblivious to her presence. Finally, she gave in and let sleep overtake her.

#

Later, when the shadows became long and dusk began to settle in Katie sat at the small kitchen table while Chase prepared supper. Jake padded in and settled against Katie's feet, trapping her at the table.

"I think he likes you." Chase said, with a ghost of a smile.

Her grey eyes met his. They hold a smile and a challenge. He returned his attention to what he was doing.

Katie watched him a few moments before turning to study the view outside. It had stopped snowing. What was left of the light simply lingered on the horizon, awash in pink and purple. The first star of evening twinkled in the royal blue sky left behind. She noticed tiny lights began to appear in the distance.

"How far away are those lights?" She asked.

Chase paused in his work to look out. "Across the valley. They seem closer than they are, but to get there you have to go down and back up again."

"Oh." She continued to scan the scene before her. The light was now gone. The sky was dark. They are alone with the mountains. And it was the mountains that brought her west in the first place.

She felt their complete solitude. Her emotions threatened to overwhelm her. She sighed deeply, running a hand through her hair. She felt Chase's eyes upon her but kept her face averted.

When she found her voice, she asked the question that had been on her mind all day. "When do you think we will be able to leave?"

"Well," he said as he set the table. "I've been thinking about that all day, trying to figure out what would be the best thing to do. It has stopped snowing, but I can't drive in it and you aren't strong enough to hike out. I suppose I could leave you here and go get help. They could get you out. If that's what you want," he added softly.

Katie looked up, her eyes meeting his. She was surprised at how tired he looked, at the shadows around his eyes. He was exhausted. She wanted to reach out and wipe the weariness from him. But she couldn't bring herself that close to him. He was offering her a way out, but she also heard the other, she had a choice. But what kind of choice was it?

Chase seemed to read her hesitation and indecision in her face. The weariness softened and his eyes filled with a tenderness she hadn't noticed before. He reached across the table and smoothed a strand of hair from her face. She pulled away from his touch. His fingers left a burning spot at her temple. He stopped and smiled rather ruefully. "I'm sorry."

"No," She said. "Don't be." She smiled what she meant to be a reassuring smile. "I think what you've suggested is a good alternative. I spent half the day today trying not to be anxious. It is very hard to think about how worried and upset my family must be, then there are the considerations that school starts and no one knows if I will be there and what do they do about that, and even when I get back I don't know if I will be able to work."

"I can understand that." He brought the food to the table. "You have responsibilities, commitments to keep. You don't want to let people down or hurt them. I get it, believe me. Depending on what it is like in the morning, I will get organized and we'll get you home."

"Thank you," she said softly.

That was her choice. So be it. He smiled, but his smile didn't reach his eyes, Katie noticed.

"Where is home?" Chase asked.

"Minnesota."

"Were you on vacation?"

"Yes. My brother, his friend and I were camping."

He began to eat. Now that a plan was in place for her to leave, he wanted to know more. "Tell me about yourself," he asked.

She hesitated. "I don't know where to begin, what do you want to know?"

"You work at a school, are you a teacher?" At her silence he continued, "You are worried about your family, tell me about them."

"Yes, I am a teacher," she said. "I teach history and political science at a small college in Minnesota. My parents are both alive and live on the farm I grew up on. I have one brother, John. He was with me on this trip." She paused, "I suppose he is still here, waiting to hear word."

"Tell me about growing up on a farm? I'm intrigued. I've never met anyone who actually grew up on a farm, I know plenty of people who have opinions about farming, including myself. But I don't actually know anyone."

"Well, people think growing up on a farm is romantic and I suppose in some ways it is. You're more sheltered, isolated from the world at large. But you worked. Working hard is drilled into you. I like to read, it was my ticket to somewhere else. I have a fairly active imagination to this day because of it.

But it was hard to find time for it. We all had responsibilities, starting at a very young age. Chores, seasonal work that needed to be done when the weather cooperated. So yeah, it's hard to explain really what it was like." Her voice drifted off as she sought out the distant lights of the night.

"It's not a lifestyle I would chose for myself," she brought her attention back, her eyes found his and she forced a smile. "But I have to say, it very much is a part of who I am today."

"We all are, to some extent, a part of wherever and however we grew up."

The silence was heavy for a moment. Katie stacked their dishes. "Thank you, Chase. It was a delicious dinner."

"You're welcome. Why don't you go ahead back into the other room? I'll clean up in here."

"Are you sure? I like to wash dishes."

"No, I'll get it. No matter what happens, tomorrow will be a long day and well, I'll take care of things now. It'll take me just a couple of minutes."

As she got up from the table, she concentrated on what she was doing. She was feeling stronger, but still got light headed when she stood. Her right ankle was very sore and swollen.

Chase watched her limp through the door, holding onto the door frame for support. He debated with himself for a minute, and then followed her.

When he went through the door, he was surprised to find her there and they crashed. They almost went down, but as they hit, he grabbed her and caught her fast.

She looked up at him. The startled look left his eyes and

his arms tighten around her. Their eyes held for minutes, and then he brushed the hair from her forehead. His hand moved down the side of her face. She didn't move a muscle or blink an eye. She stood there wrapped in his eyes, and when his lips touched hers she didn't hesitate. She had been kissed many times, but never had she felt like this.

After what seemed like an eternity, but was all too short, he was the one to break away, though not releasing her. "I'm sorry," he murmured.

At his words, he felt her tense up and withdraw. He pulled back so he could see her eyes. She stared back with a mixture of defiance and confusion. He brushed her hair back again and looked deeply in her eyes. He read her challenge and his hand gently moved, tracing her face to her chin.

"Katherine." He cupped her chin in his hand, forcing her to continue to look at him. "Katie, I don't know you, you don't know me. Tomorrow you'll be gone, just let it be." He touched her cheek lightly, "Okay?"

He was wrong, she thought. She did know him and he did know her. She was afraid of her emotions. She was scared to be with him, and scared to think about being gone. Yet she knew she must leave. Her defiance slipped away, sadness filling the space. She shook her head, trying to look away from him. She didn't want him to see the tears in her eyes.

"What is it? Katie?" He sat down on the couch pulling her down beside him. He turned to her. "What?" He leaned closer.

"I don't know," she whispered.

She felt his hand on her hair, gently stroking it. She didn't say anything. She waited for him to say something. When he didn't, she closed her eyes and leaned against him, filling her senses with his closeness, the security she felt being with him. Tomorrow she would leave. It was settled. She was so tired.

A log crashed in the fire bringing her out of her quiet reverie. She looked up at him. He seemed to be lost in thoughts of his own. He suddenly looked down and their eyes held, lost in the swirl of emotions revealed there. He moved toward her, and then hesitated. Just let it be, he had told her. That's what he would do. He felt her relax and he drew her even closer. She closed her eyes. In moments, she was asleep.

#

Later, Katie woke and found herself in bed. She turned her head to study his profile. She reached out to touch his face. Then she caught herself. She didn't want to wake him, she just wanted to look at him and memorize every line of his face. He seemed like a dream to her, one she didn't want to end, but she knew that it would. Did she love him? No, she couldn't, not yet, she had only met him, and since then she had been sleeping half the time. Even now, as she looked at his sleeping profile, she knew her emotions were due in part to the surroundings.

She lay back. That was the drawing point for Chase. He had saved her life. He had cared for her, held her, talked with her. She felt secure with him. The warmth she felt being with him drew her even closer. The environment was playing games with her. Hers was a situation in which the outcome was so uncertain and so hard to imagine.

No, she turned to look at him. He was a dream, and having him in her life was a wishful dream that would never come true. She studied his sleeping profile in the shadow of the moonlight. She was leaving. They had decided. She could not risk falling in love with him. When he was close, he scared her. When he kissed her, she wanted more. She also wanted to run, to avoid his eyes, to avoid the confusing mix of emotions he stirred in her.

Yet she couldn't help but reach out and touch him. His eyes opened. Those brown eyes she would remember forever. He wasn't a dream. Silently, he looked at her, as if she were a part of his dream. He reached for her and kissed her gently on the top of her head, pulling her against him as he did. Then was asleep again. He would probably not even remember it in the morning. But she would remember it the rest of her life for she had felt that light touch of his lips all the way down to her toes. She would leave in the morning. She closed her eyes, snug and warm in his arms and she slept, for what she supposed to be the last time, in the refuge in the mountains.

#

Someone was lifting her, she was floating through the air, then she landed on a soft cloud. Then she was lifted again and she could feel a strong arm holding her in the air. She leaned back against it, she felt a wind gently blowing against her face, slowly she drifted along, then all seemed to swirl before her and the arm was gone.

She was alone, flying through space. She could see the earth below rushing at her. She put her hands out . . .

Katie sat up with a jerk. She was gasping for breath and the room seemed to swirl all around. Hands reached for her and Chase gently held her, stroking her hair and murmuring in her ear. Gradually the spinning stopped and she caught her breath. Things in the room began to focus as she became aware of the arms which held her.

She felt flushed and disoriented, but a deep sense of security steadied her. She clung to him tightly, all plans of leaving gone. She forgot the dull pain that had been with her since the first day she had awakened in this cabin. All she was conscious of was being with Chase. She leaned back to look at his face, into his eyes. She reached up to trace the line of his jaw with her hand, his forehead and back down. He caught her hand in his and pressed it to his lips. Then he smiled. "You know," he said, kissing her hand, "you did that earlier."

He remembered. Katie pulled him to her. She wanted to remember the touch of his lips.

5

Five

"You really should get some communication equipment up there, Chase," said Tom Skerritt, the head of the Forest Service's search and rescue team. "It would have saved us a lot of time, effort and expense."

"I know. I came as soon as I could. I've lived there a long time and this is the first time this has happened," Chase said, "I'll think about it."

He was tired, his feet were sopping wet and so were the bottom of his pants. He had left at first light, following the track that passed for a road to his cabin. On a good day, he could drive it. The problem was there hadn't been a good day since he found Katherine, Katie. So he had to hike out. Once he got to the forest service road, he walked several miles before he found a group of searchers. They immediately radioed in to headquarters and took him down to the command center. Everything was in motion now to go back up and bring her down. It was the beginning of the end. It was for the best, he knew, but he also knew he wouldn't be the same. Beyond that he didn't want to think about it. He concentrated on the task at hand, to get back to the cabin and bring Katie out.

There wasn't enough snow to take snowmobiles back up. Chase thought a helicopter might be able to land, but the forest service didn't want to risk it, especially if Katie's situation wasn't life-threatening. In the end, Chase agreed to take four wheelers up.

#

Katie woke to sunlight streaming through the window. She stirred to look around the room for Chase. She felt the chill of the cabin on her nose. The fire must have gone out. It was then she realized that she was alone. Chase must have left, just as he had promised. Today she would begin the journey home.

Katie heard the roar of the four-wheelers before they came into sight. She had found Chase's note by the coffee maker, telling her what she already knew. Katie had eaten a light breakfast and then cleaned up the kitchen. She took a long shower, made the bed and waited. Chase had left Jake behind and he was good company. Now, it was time to leave. She felt a touch of anxiety about what would happen next.

And then Chase was at the door, followed by a couple of EMT's. "Ready?" He asked. She didn't trust herself to speak, so she simply nodded. "They have to check you out first before we can head out," Chase was explaining. Katie barely heard and answered the EMT's questions and let them look at her ankle, head and ribs. When they were satisfied she wasn't critically injured, they had her sign some papers before signaling they could leave.

"Do you have everything?" Chase asked.

"Yes." She shrugged, grabbing her daypack. Katie looked around the sunlit room one last time then let him help her out the door. She leaned into him more than she needed to. But she needed to. She had grown used to having his strength and it strengthened her. It was a glorious bright day, the snow was melting and the ground was soft underfoot. "We need to do this," she said. "It is time."

He nodded and said, "Just so you know, when you get down, what to expect, there will be media. You've been gone, there's been a search and it's been a slow news week. I'll do what I can to help, but it could be a circus."

"What do I need to do?"

"You don't need to do anything, let the hospital or the forest service issue a statement about the situation. If you stay silent, the story should go away. Others can run interference for you. If you want to say something, then think about what you want to say."

"Okay," she said, feeling even more overwhelmed, "I'll think about it. Thanks for the warning."

He moved his arm around her, pulling her against him for a moment, causing her to look up. He was dirty and haggard and his eyes were weary. "I'm sorry," he said. He hesitated, seeming to struggle with what he wanted to say.

She reached up and gently touched his mouth with her finger tips. "I'm sorry too," she said. "Thank you for everything you've done for me." This was their first good-bye. There wasn't a lot more to say.

Chase helped her onto the four-wheeler and then took the wheel. She wrapped her arms around him, savoring again his strength. As they drove away and headed down the mountainside, she didn't question the tears that were blinding her.

His hand closed over hers and squeezed it for a second, offering what little comfort he could. But they couldn't go back. There was nothing left to say. She looked up at the mountain behind her. So much had happened since she had first seen it. The tears subsided. She was now filled with an empty sense of loss.

The sun was long gone when Katie was finally left alone at the hotel next to the airport in Medford. She was so exhausted. Chase was right. When they reached the main road, an ambulance waited for her along with several news crews. There were reporters and cameras everywhere. Chase kept her close and rescue personnel provided protection. On the way down, she had decided she had nothing to say. She was extremely grateful, but her gratitude was targeted toward one person and she had already thanked him.

Chase rode with her to the Medford hospital. He stayed with her and helped answer more questions. The emergency room staff checked her injuries and did an assessment of her physical condition. They decided to do an x-ray of her ankle because of the continued swelling, even though she could walk on it. They determined that it was definitely sprained, but healing. They gave her a soft cast to provide support and a set of crutches to help her with the journey home.

Her ribs were bruised, not broken, which she already knew because she could breathe normally.

They looked at the bruise on the side of her head and asked questions about how long she had been unconscious and how she responded when she woke up. They double checked her reflexes and determined they didn't need to do any additional tests. But told her not to be alone for the next couple of weeks or at least until the tenderness had gone down and she felt stronger.

John arrived in the middle of all this, his relief at seeing her giving way to shock at her condition. "Katie," he said as he hugged her gently. "We have been so worried about you. Are you okay? You look terrible."

"Thanks," she said. "I feel better than I look. You called mom and dad, let them know?"

"Yes," he said. "I feel so bad. I should have insisted on going with you. I knew you were in trouble. I'm so sorry. It is my fault."

Chase came back through the curtain in time to hear his apology.

"You knew she was in trouble and you let her go alone? Didn't you realize how dangerous this mountain is?" His anger came quickly.

"John, this is Chase Harrington. He found me, saved me

and brought me here," Katie cut him off. "It is not your fault. I insisted I was okay, didn't I?"

"She did," John told Chase. "But we decided to wait about five minutes and follow her. We thought we would catch up to her along the way, but we never did. It wasn't until we got back to the trail head and camp that we realized she was missing. It was dark by the time we notified authorities. We've been searching now for four days. Thanks for what you did." He turned his attention back to Katie, "What's the situation here? Do they need to keep you or are you free to go? Mom and Dad are anxious to get you home, so Jason is checking into flights for tomorrow, so if we can we'd like to be able to leave here yet today. We'll get you on a flight and then Jason and I will drive back, straight through."

As he was laying out his plans, Katie sought out Chase. "I think we're waiting for the final word," she said. "Chase?"

"Right, they're doing their final assessment and preparing whatever paper work needs to be completed. I get the impression you will be cleared to leave."

Shortly after that she was told she could go. John turned to leave but Chase held back. This was it, she knew. This was good-bye. She watched him approach and she lost herself once more in the depths of his eyes. He leaned over and kissed her softly, tenderly and quickly. Leaving just a taste, a remembrance of what had been, what might have been. "I'm going to leave you now," he said. "Good-bye. Take care of yourself."

"Good-bye," she said, "And thank you again, for everything."

"Any time you're in need of rescuing, just let me know, I'll be there." He smiled, but the smile didn't reach his eyes.

"I'll do that," she said, trying to be light hearted too, despite the fact her heart was actually breaking.

He kissed her again, and then was gone.

The drive to the hotel seemed to take forever. She wished she could have another day of rest, but John and Jason were anxious to start the drive back. Tomorrow she would be home.

Despite her exhaustion, she couldn't fall asleep. Pictures of Chase kept getting in the way. Finally, weariness won and sleep stole the pictures from her. She woke once and reached for Chase. He wasn't there. She sat up with a start, disoriented. Then she remembered. She lay staring at the ceiling for a long time. Then she reached for the other pillow and curled around it. Eventually, sleep came again and the tears dried on her cheeks for the last time.

6

Chapter Six

In the winter of my heart
i found the strength to stand time
alone.
Cold and wind swirl around.
On the air floats a song.
Memories seep through to warm me
as i felt that old familiar pain.
Weaker i turn
looking again,
i need you.

Katie Carlson and her dog, Misty, were almost done with their three-mile run. The snow swirled around her, wetting her face and freezing her eye lids together. She blinked and could see again. She opened her mouth to eat some of the fresh cold snow. Nothing in the world could compare to running in Minnesota at five degrees above zero. She was hot under all her layers of cold weather gear. She pulled the scarf up around her mouth again. Her hands were getting sweaty, but she left the mittens on for she knew if she removed them they would get cold.

Katie began running almost immediately upon returning from Oregon. She did so in part to restore her strength and stamina but also as a release from time and her thoughts. It was the only time she let herself think of Chase and what might have been. Misty provided companionship and quiet moral support.

Katie fought to forget Chase Harrington. She was disciplined, independent and determined. She knew in her head it was best to put the whole experience behind her, but those dark eyes continued to haunt her dreams.

Katie reached the driveway, her stopping point. She walked past the mailboxes and started down the hill. She could see the yard light shining through the swirling whiteness giving each snow flake a glow of its own. The stars couldn't be seen. Yet, there was a soft glow beyond the cloudy snow quietly lighting the fields as they turned from black to white. The morning would dawn fresh, crisp and white. A new year.

Tonight was New Year's Eve. Katie was surprised she was looking forward to it. She had a date. Originally, she didn't have any plans for the evening, but Neil asked her out for the evening. He was an old friend from high school. Their friendship was old enough that she knew him well and she knew he wanted more from her than friendship. She knew he felt friendship was enough to build a life around. But she had decided long ago she would rather live her life alone than live it with a man she didn't love. She knew that's what she wanted. She wasn't going to go looking for love, if she found it along the way, that was another thing altogether. And after her experience with Chase, she remained convinced.

Katie heard her Dad doing chores and went to the cattle yard. "Hi Dad" She said cheerfully. "How are the cattle doing?" They all looked so soft and cuddly with their long winter coats, the steam coming from their nostrils and their soft brown eyes questioning. Their eyes reminded her of Jake. No, she shook her head.

"Good, I'm almost done here," Alex Carlson answered. "Do you want to hang out while I finish. I need to do hay and check their water."

"Sure, I need to cool down before going inside."

Alex Carlson knew something had changed in his strong, independent daughter. Something more than just the physical injuries. There was more to her story, but he knew he no longer could press her for details about her life. He was just glad she decided to be at home for a while to recover.

"Dad, remember when John and I were little we had that one pet cow?"

He stepped over the fence down from the feed bunk. He shook his head and smiled at her. "I sure do, Katie. You guys were so little then. I remember the day he almost butted me out of the feed bunk. He sure was a frisky little steer. I was so mad that day, he was lucky I didn't shoot him on the spot. But he grew out of it."

"Oh yeah, I remember that too. When he got bigger he forgot us, still I was sad the day you took him away."

"That's farming."

"Yep, something no one understands. And the hours we built forts in the hay mow are something few kids today experience," Katie said as they went together into the barn.

"A lot has changed since you kids were little. A lot in farming has changed. But one thing that hasn't is the 24/7 work week."

"True. There's always work to be done. But I've found a lot of jobs are like that, just different."

"I suppose, I wouldn't know."

"Or maybe, it's because all I ever knew was work that work still seems that way. It's funny to feel old already."

"You're not old. Things have a way of changing us. There are some days when I feel so young and other days when I feel ancient, worn out, older than I actually am. Life is strange that way. I guess that's what makes it interesting."

"I know, but right now it's really hard." She was as close to tears as ever Chase's face was vivid. She could see the half smile quietly comforting her.

It was the most she had said to her parents about her situation. She knew they were curious but she really couldn't talk about it.

"Well, it's a new year tomorrow and you have plans for tonight. My best advice, enjoy the evening and start fresh tomorrow." He gave her a smile that was meant to be encouraging.

Later she pulled the brush through her hair one more time. When the doorbell rang she liked the way she looked. When she had looked into the mirror in the hospital in Oregon, she had quite a surprise. She had no idea she looked so awful. Now her blond hair was shinny and full, the light catching it here and there created burnish highlights. Her skin was smooth and clear. She wore a little makeup.

Tonight she looked beautiful and felt beautiful. Too bad it was for Neil and not Chase. She shrugged. She was done thinking about Chase for today, she told herself. She took one more look in the mirror, smoothed down her dress and went down stairs.

Neil stood as she came down the last couple steps. "Hi," she said and smiled. He looked nice. His blond unruly hair was combed and he had on a dark blue suit that accentuated his blue eyes. "Ready?"

Neil was silent on their way to town. It had stopped snowing, leaving a light cover on everything. It was a beautiful night. She looked up at the full moon. There were the stars which had been hidden before. She couldn't help but reflect that there were not nearly as many stars here as there had been in Oregon. She brought her eyes to earth again and looked out over the rolling farm land. There were groups of trees dotting the countryside where farmers and their families lived. It was peaceful and quiet.

She looked sideways at Neil. He looked nice. "Did you have a good Christmas?" She asked breaking the silence.

He turned his eyes back to the road. "Yes, I did. It was just the family, my sister and her husband with their two little girls."

Picking up on the little girls she asked him about them and they continued to talk about his family until they reached the restaurant. She was surprised to see where they were dinning. The Rosewood Inn was a romantic evening spot. It was situated on the edge of the lake with a gorgeous view. "Oh, Neil, how nice" she said as they pulled up. "I love this place."

He turned and took her hand in his. She flushed at the intensity of his gaze. He didn't smile, shortly he said, "I'm glad. I've never been here. But it was recommended to me by my neighbor's wife." He paused and continued to regard her with his serious blue eyes. "Did I tell you? You are beautiful tonight."

She smiled at him, "No you didn't, but thank you. Hey," she said, "come on." She released his hand and opened the car door, "I'm starving. I ran three miles this afternoon. It was great with the snow swirling all around. It was like being in your own little world."

A festive feeling permeated the Inn. "Isn't it beautiful?" She said, smiling up at him. She caught his arm and hugged it. "Come on, relax, let's enjoy ourselves." She was determined to have a good time and Neil was going to enjoy himself too. There was no reason not to, she told herself.

The atmosphere, good food and wine began to work their magic. Maybe she really could forget Oregon tonight. Neil wasn't the same Neil she had known all her life. He began to relax and talk more freely. He even touched her hand now and again. He was an entirely different person. They had been friends since forever, but as they had gotten older the friendship was strained as he had made it clear he wanted more. As a result, she hadn't spent time with him in a very long time.

The Inn was crowded as more couples came to dance in the New Year. She looked at them, laughing with each other, excitement glowing in their eyes. She became painfully aware again of the emptiness inside. I am enjoying myself, a voice told her.

They sat for a time in companionable silence, watching the dancing. Katie's thoughts were a mixture and she drifted. When Neil touched her hand she almost jumped, startled. For a moment she didn't know where she was and she saw a pair of dark eyes watching her intently. She shook her head and the brown eyes were replaced by a set of intensely blue ones. She smiled at him. "Sorry, I was in another world for a minute."

He didn't say anything. She looked away and watched the dancing again. Misinterpreting her gaze, he asked, "Do you want to dance?"

"Okay," she shrugged.

He led her to the floor and took her in his arms. He held her close, but she felt awkward and misplaced. They danced for what seemed ages. The music for the most part was slow and romantic. It didn't help. The longing she felt inside wasn't diminishing; in fact it was growing stronger the more she tried to bury it. She needed to do something to take her mind off of Chase. He was not hers. He had never been hers, except, perhaps for the few moments when he held her. She needed to bring herself back to the present.

"Hey, listen," she said, "Can we take a break?"

"Sure," he said. "Would you like something to drink? Dessert?"

"Another glass of wine would be perfect."

They ordered their drinks and sat for a few minutes in companionable silence. Their table was situated by a window with a view of the lake. Katie looked out the window at the still night. The lake was beautiful. The moon was full and the fresh snow looked soft and bright. Without meaning to her mind was transported across the country and she was in a small cabin in Oregon and the stars were bright and the view breathtaking.

"What are you thinking about?"

Katie jumped. "Oh. What?" She asked, abruptly brought back to the present. This was getting old, this drifting away.

"Boy," he said. "I'm not sure you're even here tonight."

"I'm sorry," she said with a rueful smile. "What did you ask me?"

"I asked you what you were thinking about."

"Oh," she paused, wondering how much to say. "Well, I was thinking how beautiful it is out on the lake tonight. It reminds me of the time I spent in Oregon this fall. The nights looked very similar. Except, of course, there were many more stars there."

She saw his questioning look and answered. "It's simple. There weren't any street lights around to dim their beauty. We get so used to the ambient lights, we don't even know what we're missing."

"You really miss Oregon, don't you?" He asked.

"Yes, I do." She paused again. He sat waiting, waiting, she knew for a longer answer. An answer to why; why did she miss Oregon? She didn't know what more to say. There was so much she missed.

He reached across the table and took her hand. She was surprised by his gentle touch. She was warmed by it. "Something happened there, didn't it?" He asked.

She opened her mouth and hesitated, not knowing what to say. But he waved his hand. "I know about the accident. Who didn't? It was all over the news. Until you were found, that is. No one really knows much beyond that. But your Dad told me you have been struggling since you got back."

"What?"

"I asked him about you in October, just in conversation. I knew you had had an accident, that you had been lost for several days. Or at least we thought you were lost. But then you're found and news died out. When I asked your Dad what happened he told me you had cracked a couple of ribs and some other injuries. But something more happened. You've changed."

At her look of surprise, he added, "We maybe haven't seen each other for a few years, but I've known you my entire life. You can pretend, but I'm not sure you can hide." He smiled and looked down and gently took her hand. Of course, she should have known. If the tables had been turned, she would have known too.

She looked out the window across the lake at the full moon, trying to collect her thoughts. "Neil, please understand. I don't remember the accident. A lot happened to me out there I can't explain. I'd rather not talk about it. There's a lot I'm trying to deal with and often it catches me unaware. Okay?"

"Of course. If you need someone to talk to, though, I'll be happy to listen."

She gave him a half smile to say thank you. They sat a moment longer before the band struck up Auld Lange Sine. Without a word he pulled her up and into his arms. She leaned against him and slipped her arms around his neck. At the end of the dance he held her and gently kissed her. Then the whole place went wild as the band struck up a fast one. They stayed and danced a while, laughing and enjoying themselves. Their friendship was renewed.

Finally, exhausted, they left. As they were getting in the car he asked her if she wanted to go for a walk on the lake. She hesitated, and then said yes. They drove away from the bright lights and noise of the Inn to a little park close by and parked the car.

He took her hand in his as they started out across the snow-covered lake. They walked in companionable silence. After a little way they stopped and looked around, in wonder of a winter night.

"It's beautiful out here." He spoke softly and turned to face her. She could read it in his eyes, she knew what was coming, yet, when his lips touched hers she was surprised. She did not get lost in the kiss and it seemed he held her tightly for an eternity. She tried to kiss him back, but her heart was not in it. Finally, he drew away. "I'm sorry," he said, dropping his arms. He drew a long breath as though trying to steady the emotions flowing through him.

After an awkward silence, he began to walk back across the snow towards the car. She didn't move. This was not a good ending.

"Neil, wait!" She ran after him. He stopped and waited for her.

"Neil, I'm sorry. I didn't mean . . ." She stopped in mid-sentence.

"I know you didn't. That's just it." He shrugged and looked out across the lake. Then he looked directly at her, the pain clear in his eyes. He spoke softly, "I don't have a chance, do I?"

She opened her mouth to speak but he cut her off. "No, don't say you're sorry. You've nothing to be sorry for. It's my fault. You can't be blamed for not feeling the way I want you to feel. I kept hoping, always hoping that you might fall in love with me. But it's not your fault that you didn't live up to my expectations." He stared off at the stars. She waited for him to continue. He looked back at her. " Katie, can we still be friends?"

She took his arm and started leading him back to the car. "Neil, I'm sorry. I'm not entirely back to normal and am very unsure of myself. But we've always been friends, I'd like that to continue."

Neil dropped her off around 2 a.m. After leaving the lake they went to an all-night restaurant and had a cup of hot chocolate to warm them. They talked about unimportant things. And it was nice.

Nice, that's what Katie thought as she watched Neil drive away. That's all it was. Nice. It was fun, too, she decided. Something different than anything she had done on New Year's Eve in a while. She didn't feel like going to bed yet. She went in the house and changed clothes putting on old jeans and a heavy jacket. Back outside she took the two dogs, Skippy and Misty, and headed out around the grove.

A cold wind blew through to her bones. It was a clear January night. The stars twinkled above her and she hunched her shoulders deeper into her coat. She looked out over the snow-covered fields so plainly lit in the moonlight without seeing them. Instead she saw a face, a faced lined with weariness, the brown eyes full of concern and then tenderness. Chase. She couldn't believe how much she missed him. She knew she would never forget him, but she had never expected to feel so lost. The memory faded as she saw how bleak and lonely the land looked under the moonlight. Looking upon the stillness she felt as though she fit in with the scenery. Her heart was as cold as the wind, her eyes as misty as her breath and she felt as bleak as the countryside in which she walked.

She sighed wearily and looked for a place to sit. She didn't care if she stayed out all night. It was cold, but she had dressed for it. She found a log that wasn't covered with snow and sat down. She didn't know how long she sat there. She let her mind wander. At length a certain measure of peace came to her. She got up and stretched. She was beginning to feel the cold. Her toes were starting to turn numb.

She called to the dogs, but they had abandoned her long ago. The snow drifts prevented her from going any further around the back of the grove so she turned around and walked down the driveway. When she reached the end, she stopped and turned around. The place was quiet and sleeping. She could see the night beginning to fade around the edges of the horizon and decided at last it was time to go inside.

She stopped, awed, and watched a star slowly fall through the early morning light. She made a wish, perhaps it was a futile wish, but it came without thought. Then she went inside. She was cold and tired.

7

Seven

Rain was falling gently as I hurried up the long hill to Grandpa's house. Drawing near I could see the lights from the windows and smell the warmth of the fire. Opening the door I stepped into the light of the kitchen, the smell of supper accosted my nose.

"Hi, smells good." Quickly I hung up my rain coat, pulled a comb through the wet tangles asking, "Can I do anything?"

"No, it's all ready. Did you have a good day?" Grandma asked as she ladled the hot soup into the bowls.

"Well, welcome home Katie!" Grandpa boomed, giving me a hug and a fond kiss when he came in the room. "Did you have a good day out in the boat? How was the ocean today It looked a little rough?"

When we sat down Grandpa asked the blessing on the food and then turned to me. "So, Katie, tell us about your day. You look a little dreamy and sleepy." He chided with a teasing note in his voice.

"No comment." I smiled . . .

Puffing, my hands swollen from exertion and cold, I looked up the trail to watch him climb ahead. Stopping, he turned around, and waited for me with a smile. He shouted, "Just a little farther. You're doing great."

When I reached the point where he waited he pulled me close and gave me a tender kiss. Looking down at me he grinned. "I love you." I melted inside when he looked at me. Those dark eyes full of love made me realize how lucky I was to have him and how much I loved him. . .

Sipping my wine I looked out the window to the rocky coast below. As my eyes misted up, he reached across the small table for my hand. "Are you okay?" He asked, his dark eyes full of love and concern. I smiled slowly, "I'm trying to understand the wonder of it all. . ."

The blinding white on the mountain caused me to squint as I paused to look down. Someone swept by leaving me in a swirl of snow. From the way he moved, I could tell who it was. Shouting at him I pushed off. He was waiting at the bottom with a grin on his face. He picked me up and threw me in the snow. I got what I wanted . . .

We sat staring quietly into the dying embers of the campfire, lost in memories of the day. As the fire lost its warmth, I snuggled closer to him. Eventually we pulled ourselves away from the hypnotic flames, each immersed in thoughts. "Good night," he said as he headed for his sleeping bag. I nodded silently and slid into my bag. Later, upon hearing his footsteps I opened my eyes and sat up. He bent to kiss me. "I love you," was all he said . . .

Katie's alarm clock went off at ten. She rolled over and shut it off. She couldn't get up. She was having a wondrous dream. She wanted it to go on forever. She determinedly closed her eyes and cuddled deeper under the covers. Sleep came again, but it was without dreams.

She came awake slowly. She turned over and opened her eyes to look at the clock. It was 1 p.m. She pushed her hair back and struggled to wake up.

Suddenly John burst into the room. He came over and sat down on the bed. He surveyed her for a moment, "You look awful. How late did you stay out, anyway?"

"Thanks." She gave him a dirty look. She didn't want him disturbing her. The early morning dream was still warm. She pushed her hair back off her face. She was tired, stiff and sore from sitting out in the cold.

He continued to look at her with a questioning expression. "Well," he drawled. "Did you have fun with Neil?" He emphasized Neil in the tone of voice younger brothers use when they want to bug an older sister.

"You're bad."

"I'm sorry." He grinned. The smile left his face. "But really. What happened? Did you have a good time?"

At the doubt in her face he added, "Or was it a bummer."

"Well, no. It was fun. Except near the end, it was awkward." She shook her head. "I don't know, anyway, it was fine," she paused, and changed the subject. "What's on the agenda for the day?"

John stood up to leave the room. "That's what I came up to tell you. We're going to go ice skating pretty soon and I thought you'd like to come."

She scrambled out of bed. "How soon are you going? Will you wait for me?"

"Sure, we wouldn't go without you." With that he left and she hurried into her long underwear, sweater and jeans. She could always count on John to figure out a way to make her feel better. He knew, of course, most of what had happened to her in Oregon. He was the only one who had actually met Chase. Even so, she had kept what happened between them to herself. But John knew something had happened. He knew Katie hadn't been the same since she returned to Minnesota all those months ago. He probably knew her better than anyone else. He gave her the space she needed. But he was always looking for ways to keep her from spending too much time alone, with her thoughts.

Later, out on the lake, Katie pushed all the air out of her cheeks and watched as it condensed into its own little cloud. It was a beautiful day. The colors of the sky, the trees, the dead winter grasses, the spots of remaining snow were sharp as a picture in the cold clear air. She circled around on her skates and looked back across the lake. The old bridge over the creek was gone. In its place was a large culvert. It didn't look the same from this angle, but she supposed the farmers needed the broadening in order to get their large machinery through. She looked around for the others. They were over by the park playing tag or crack the whip. She watched them some moments then continued on her solitary way.

She was in high spirits. She had slept well and the early morning dreams lingered. She skated along the bumpy ice, sometimes pushing hard, other times going slowly. She drifted from the center of the lake to the edges and snooped around in the tall grasses that grew there. Nothing stirred. The small birds and animals that lived in the marshy weeds were hidden from the winter cold. She found an empty nest, abandoned long ago when the ducks or geese or whoever occupied it had flown south. They were smart, she thought, fleeing the cold and still death of winter for the warmth and life of the sun.

When danger threatened, animals could blend in with the scenery or die. But humans, she thought, we have to live through all the trials we encounter. We could try to hide, but we'd feel it anyway. And to die would be the coward's way out. If she would have thought about it sooner, running from one's emotions and feelings were just as cowardly.

She suddenly sat down in some weeds. What had she done? What had she left behind in Oregon? Questions churned through her head. The good feeling was gone, replaced by one of bewilderment. She felt an enormous sense of loss. But how was I to know I would feel this way when I left, she questioned. She knew she would miss him. But what she hadn't realized was that she had actually fallen in love with him. She had rationalized the feelings away. And now, now on a winter's day in Minnesota, the full realization of what she felt hit her. And she had walked away from it. She didn't talk to him about all the conflicting emotions she felt. No, she just went with the mood. And then she walked away. Instead of admitting she loved him, she fought it and ultimately left. What an idiot!

She laid her head on her knees and hugged them to herself. The tears came unchecked. Oh, what had she done? She felt so lost and alone.

January twilight was coming on. She could hear everyone laughing with each other in the distance. She started back. Her tears had solved nothing, but she felt better. As she skated in the fading light she knew she would always love Chase.

She saw John break away from the rest of their friends. She wiped her eyes but he took one look at her and knew she had been crying. He grabbed her arm and swung her around so that she was skating backwards. He pushed and soon they were going incredibly fast over the rough ice. Then he ground his skates in and they went into a fast spin that left them dizzy and breathless. John was grinning broadly at her. She couldn't help but feel better. His craziness was infectious. "John, what are you trying to do to me?" She reached out for support.

He started laughing and she joined in. "You loved it. Besides, now no one else can tell you were crying." He took her hand and they skated together in silence back to the others. Then he gave her a shove, "You're it," and skated away from her, and so did everyone else.

Katie laughed, "Thanks a lot," and proceeded to try to tag someone.

#

It was a snowy morning in February. The weekly storm was just beginning. Katie could feel the north wind's breath blowing against the house. She reached for the clock, 7 a.m. It was cold outside the covers and she turned on the radio and snuggled down into them again. The forecast was gloomy. Snow all day and all the next. Wearily she crawled out of bed and pulled her robe around her and slipped on her down house boots. She walked to the kitchen and turned on the coffee, let Misty out to take care of her business and went back to stare out the window. The morning light was muted by the swirling snow and it seemed earlier than 7 a.m. She stared at the white mass churning before her. There was snow piled in the yard from the previous storms and the drifts were beginning to form on top of them. It looked like she would be snowed in for the weekend. Great, she was so tired of being snowed in. There had been storms every week since school started.

The coffee was done and she took her cup and walked through the house. She was going to go crazy. The last month had been so long. She sat on the couch in the living room and put her head in her hands.

School had started several weeks ago. She was teaching four courses. She had two sections of U.S. History 110, each containing fifty freshmen and a sprinkling of upperclassmen. Most of them were taking it as a requirement and didn't really care. She tried to make the class as interesting as possible, in hopes that they would learn something valuable.

She also taught a course in American Intellectual History. She demanded a lot out of her students in this course. She traced the intellectual foundations of the United States; Rousseau, Locke, Hume and others, as well as studied contemporary intellectual ideas such as Darwinism, Freud, and Marxism. Although many of the philosophers they studied were not American, the emphasis was on how their ideas shaped American history. It was a history course, not philosophy. She was trying to teach the kids the ideas that lie behind much of the action in history and what to look for in evaluating the events of the day. She tried to refrain from lecturing too much and left room for discussion. Usually she'd give an introductory lecture on a man or idea, then they'd discuss what they had read on the subject. She didn't give her students all the answers to the questions they studied. She wanted them to think for themselves. She didn't give tests, only pop quizzes on the reading. In addition, each student had to give a presentation on a man or idea plus a ten to fifteen-page paper.

As much as she liked this class, her favorite was the one she taught on contemporary affairs. This gave her a chance to keep up on current issues and read new books. It was in preparing for this class that she had first heard of Chase Harrington. She had selected his book on land use the first year she taught. That was two years ago.

As it was the first book they read, they had already covered it in class for this semester. It had been hard leading the discussion, for she learned much about Chase in rereading the book. His thoughts on land use related directly to his thoughts on relationships. He argued that attitudes toward people, animals and things are personified in the way they care for the earth. She reflected on how she had thought his cabin appeared to have been looked after and well maintained. She remembered how he cared for her, gently holding her when she was afraid, catching her when she almost fell, and picking her up when she did fall. She realized it was in his character to care for her the way he did. He treated her the way he would have treated anyone he found in her condition at the bottom of a mountain gully. She couldn't explain his kisses, but she was almost convinced they didn't mean he was in love with her.

She got up and looked out the window at the snow flying. She was so tired of the snow. The day loomed. She had gone out with friends the night before but had no special plans for the rest of the weekend. Despite her school schedule, she felt she had too much time on her hands. She wanted to keep busy and so tried to keep an active schedule, but this weekend stretched before her empty. She had started a couple of projects for these times, but it was always an effort to get motivated. She was sewing a quilt by hand. But while she sewed her mind would dart about and then she had to quit and try to do something else, something to keep the memory of Chase at bay.

The memory hadn't lessened and his face would pop into

her mind at the most unexpected moments. The end of the day, when she closed her eyes for the night was the worst time of all. She remembered the feeling of being held securely in his arms. Instead of pushing that particular memory away, she had learned to embrace it, relax and sleep. But the daylight hours were a different matter altogether.

A scratching noise brought her out of her depressing thoughts. She went to the door and there was Misty, waiting to come in out of the cold. She opened the door and the puppy rushed in, bringing the snow and cold air with her. "Misty!" She laughed. Misty jumped up and tried to lick her face. "Get down until you're dried off." She poured herself a second cup of coffee, got out a piece of paper and sat at the table.

8

Eight

Later that same day Katie pushed herself away from her desk and stretched. She felt satisfied. The day had passed fairly quickly. On her desk lay the beginnings of a new book of poetry. It was a compiling of the poetry she had written in the past year. Much of it had been written before the trip to Oregon and a few pieces after she returned.

She had spent the morning baking bread and doing household chores. The activity helped lift her spirits. Then she showered and sat down at her desk to see what she needed to do for work. She read some quiz papers and graded them. But soon she was finished.

Still feeling pensive she took out the journal where she kept her poems. After reading through them, she decided to type them up on her computer and organize them. Now the task was to polish them off before sending them to her publisher. It looked like she had another book in the making. The thought excited her.

She went into the kitchen and made fresh coffee. Misty stirred sleepily in her corner when she heard the water run. While she waited for the coffee to brew she looked out the window at the dusk. The violence of the snowstorm no longer depressed her. She decided to take Misty and go out. They had been cooped up so much of the winter. The fresh air would be good for them both. She thought of the work sitting on her desk, but it wasn't priority. Putting on her heavy outside clothes, they went out into the storm.

She couldn't see much in the fading light and swirling snow, but she could feel the snow biting into her exposed face. She pulled the scarf up around her mouth and nose and pulled her stocking cap lower until only her eyes were showing. The snow was piling up into huge drifts. She started a game of tag with Misty and soon was laughing and falling down into the snow. After a few minutes they were both tired and cold. As they neared the door, she could hear the phone ringing.

Katie burst into the house and grabbed the phone. "Hello?" She said breathlessly.

"Hello, Katherine?" A deep male voice asked.

"Yes?"

"This is Steve Jackson."

"Oh?" Steve Jackson? Who was Steve Jackson? The name sounded familiar to her but she knew they had never met. He had an alluring voice and her curiosity was aroused.

He hesitated. "We haven't met, I'm new in town. I moved here last October. I'm an attorney with the Legal Services Department downtown."

Now she knew where she had heard of him. He had been suggested as a possible speaker for her Contemporary Affairs class on social-legal issues and the work of the Legal Services Department. But they hadn't reached that part in the class yet. She wondered what he wanted. "What can I do for you?"

"Well, the reason I'm calling is that Stan Coleman told me you teach a class on Contemporary Affairs at the college."

"That's right."

"He told me some of the details about what you teach and I thought perhaps you would be interested in the work of the Legal Services Department."

"Well, to tell you the truth, Steve, I am. But that section doesn't come up until later this semester. So, there's plenty of time. If you'll give me your number or email, I'll contact you around the first of April and we'll line up a definite time then. Okay?"

The line remained silent.

"Is there something wrong?"

Steve didn't answer right away.

"No, nothing's wrong," he hesitated for a second before plunging ahead. "I was wondering if you were free to have coffee next Saturday morning. I was going to call for today, but the forecast was for more snow and then this morning, sure enough there was the snow."

"I really don't know. What did Stan tell you?"

He hesitated again, "Not much. I don't know very many people here and so when he suggested I call you I thought it might be a good idea. He thought we might have a few things in common, and so I thought coffee would be good."

"Oh. . ." Katie paused. "I don't know. I usually have a pretty full list of things to do on Saturday mornings. Let me think about it, okay?"

"I wasn't asking you out on a date, just a cup of coffee."

"I don't know right now," she insisted. "Let's touch base later in the week." She slammed the phone down and leaned against the wall.

Slowly she undid her long scarf and took off her outerwear. She couldn't believe what just happened. It was so unexpected. He was so pushy. He had a nice voice, her thoughts trailed off. She pushed herself away from the wall angrily. She couldn't be expected to go out with every single man that crossed her path. She didn't want to see anyone yet anyway. What did it matter? She would call him in April and ask him to speak to her class. Maybe then they could have coffee and talk about it.

She went upstairs, ran a hot bath and pushed all thoughts of Steve Jackson out of her mind. Flashes of Chase came to mind and she felt them for a moment then willed them out of her life. She needed to stop dwelling on him and get on with living. He was past, over. She would never see him again, nor think of him.

That night she worked on her book of poems. She drank cup after cup of coffee. And when she saw the light beginning to creep over the horizon, she ate. Then she went to bed.

Monday morning dawned bright and crisp. The snow had been cleared and there was no excuse to stay home. Katie felt dragged out and exhausted from pulling her all-nighter on Saturday night. But she had something she needed to do before she could start her week. She had transferred her confusion from the phone call from Steve Jackson into anger at her friend Stan Coleman. She was going to talk to him first thing this morning. He didn't stand a chance. Katie found him in his office getting ready for his first class.

"What are you doing here so early?" He asked, surprised to see her.

"I wanted to talk to you before the day and week got away from us," she said. "Did you encourage Steve Jackson to call me?"

"Oh," Stan said, leaning back in his desk chair. "So that's why you're here so early, to tell me to mind my own business. That you are fine, and to leave you alone."

"Yes, exactly," Katie fumed. "I'm fine. I've told you that before. I really don't appreciate you interfering with my personal life. If being in a relationship were a priority for me, I'd be in one. It's not. Please, Stan, don't put me into these situations."

"I'm sorry, Katie, if you think I overstepped. I like you and I like Steve. I'll leave it at that."

"Thank you, Stan, I know you mean well, but please I just need my space."

With that, she left. She said her piece, he apologized and yet the frustration and anger lingered throughout the week. She avoided him which was not easy because it was a very small school and they were part of a three-person history department.

On Thursday he stopped by her classroom at the end of her last class. "Maria and the boys wanted me to ask you over for dinner on Friday night."

Katie hesitated, she knew her anger was misdirected, but she didn't trust herself to talk about what was really going on. She'd been doing a pretty good job of avoidance. However, Stan and Maria and their family were among her closest and most trusted friends.

"Yes, of course," she finally answered. "I've missed seeing them all and I would enjoy that, thank you."

#

Friday night she went directly over to the Colemans. Stan and Maria's little boys were adorable. They were five and six, that perfect age of mischief and sweetness. Hanging out and playing with them would be a welcome respite.

After dinner, Stan and Katie relaxed in the family room while Maria was upstairs putting the boys to bed. "Listen, Katie," Stan said. "I'm sorry for suggesting Steve call you. I didn't think you would be so upset. He's a nice guy and doesn't know anyone here so I thought I would be doing you both a favor."

"I know, it's okay. I don't like surprises generally, and

lately, as you know, it's been a hard return from my accident, so it did kind of set me off."

Maria stopped further discussion on the matter as she came downstairs. Her timing was great and the subject was closed.

"Well, they're safely tucked away. Hopefully they'll be asleep in minutes so we can have some peace and quiet around here." She joined Katie on the couch. "They really do take a lot out of you in a day."

"Oh Maria! They are so much fun! But I can understand how worn out you must be at the end of the day, they take a lot of energy." Katie said. "The dinner was delicious too. You shouldn't have fussed. It's Friday night and you must be as tired as the rest of us after a full week."

"Oh, no Katie, we're so glad you could come over. It's been a while. And the meal was no effort at all. I enjoy cooking a real meal once in a while. Right, Stan?"

Stan smiled fondly at his wife in agreement.

"More coffee?" Maria leaned over and refilled her cup. "Katie, how have you been? Stan tells me you haven't been feeling well lately. You look awfully tired."

What could she say to them? They were friends. She hesitated, "I've completed a new book of poems and I've been working on them every night this week. I want to get it to my publisher as soon as I can. I've also been reading a lot for my class. We're using a new book in Contemporary Affairs and I've been trying to get a good grasp on it before the weekend. I guess I've only gotten about five hours a night of sleep, so I am pretty wiped out."

She could read the disbelief on their faces. But she didn't care. She didn't want to discuss Chase, or the accident, as she called it. Chase was a person she had put out of her mind.

The room was silent for a couple of minutes as they drank their coffee and sought a safe subject of conversation. Finally, Maria asked, "What is the book about?"

Which book? Katie took the safe way out. "It's a new work about the Israeli-Palestine conflict. It goes into the historical roots, the Biblical roots and also an in-depth analysis of the situation today as well as the outlook for the future. It's quite interesting. But there is so much in it, that it is difficult to grasp in the first reading."

Katie had Stan's interest now. Although Stan taught European history, his real interest lay with foreign affairs and historical conflicts. The Mid-East question was one of history as well as current policy. You couldn't separate one from the other.

"Who wrote it?"

"Sam Baron. Would you like to see a copy of the book? Maybe you could read it and then talk it through with me. You're more up on the Mid-East than I am. I would be grateful for your help."

"Yes. I'd love to read it. But the problem is time. When are you going to use it in class?"

"I was hoping to use it around the first of March. We'll be on it for a couple of weeks since it is almost 500 pages long. Is that enough time?"

"Well, why don't you give me a copy of it on Monday and

I'll see how it goes. I should be able to have it read and to discuss it with you by the end of the month, but I don't want to promise you anything." He paused and looked at her for a couple of minutes, as he debated how to say what was on his mind. "You're not using it until March and you've already read it once and are studying it? Aren't you a bit ahead of yourself?"

"No, it's a tough book and I want to be thoroughly familiar with it. And that time of year is hectic, you know with mid-terms and papers. I don't want to be caught unprepared."

"I've never known you to be unprepared in the two years you've taught here! What I don't understand is why you are working so hard. Why do you stay up all night working on poetry and reading books? You have always used time well. I don't know why you're suddenly losing sleep over work. Katie, you haven't been yourself this semester. You're working too hard and it's a strain on you. You're great with your students, but you can't carry whatever it is you're carrying by yourself. We're your friends. Let us help you."

"Is that what you were trying to do when you encouraged Steve Jackson to call? Help me? Come on, Stan. We already discussed this. I thought the subject was closed." She could feel the tension coil tightly in her stomach. "I appreciate your friendship. It means a lot. But I'll be alright with time. Right now, I just have to keep working. As long as I don't get sick or neglect my students I'll be fine. If I start neglecting my students, please let me know. But don't set me up with anymore men. I'm really not interested at this point."

"No, it's not okay." Stan stood up emphatically. "You're on the verge of a nervous collapse. I've never seen you like this before and Maria and I are worried about you. Who cares about your students! You've got to take care of yourself or you won't be able to teach. You can't work yourself into forgetting whatever it is you're trying to forget." He raised his hand to keep her from speaking. "No, you don't have to tell us about it. But I want to remind you we're your friends. We care about you. We're here for you. You can try to shut us out, but we're not going."

Katie felt the walls she had so carefully built crumble. It began slowly as her tension drained, her eyes filled with tears and she tried to speak, but the words wouldn't come. It all flashed before her . . . Chase's face, Jake, the cabin, the loneliness and longing she'd been desperately trying to deny.

She looked tearfully from Stan to Maria. "I'm so sorry. I've been so wrapped up in running from myself that I'm not aware of what I'm doing to others. Maybe I need to talk about it, to lay it all out on the table, to admit to myself I'm no longer the self-sufficient, independent woman I want everyone to believe I am." With that start, the whole story came tumbling out.

The room was silent for several long minutes as Stan and Maria absorbed her story. Maria was the first to speak. "We never realized, no wonder . . ." her voice trailed off.

"No I didn't either. I mean, look at the circumstances. Would you trust your emotions?"

"Yes. But I've always been comfortable with my emotions."

"You have a point. I've never been comfortable with emotion. I've always felt out of my depth. And, as you both know, it's very important for me to be in control. My whole being is centered on the image I've created of me — strong, independent, and confident. Now I'm floundering, unsure of myself and who I am. It's very disconcerting."

"Yes, I can see how it would be." Stan hesitated. "You're a lot like me in that regard. Maria has taught me a lot about being comfortable with my emotions. But it is an ongoing lesson." He went to stir the fire before asking. "Are you sure you're in love with him?"

Katie pondered the question, one she had asked herself a thousand times. "Yes." She nodded. "But where does that get me?"

"Do you think Chase fell in love with you?" Maria asked gently.

"I don't know. Sometimes when I search my memory I think so — but then I continue on and I don't know. I don't know him. I only know him in that setting and from his books. I don't have anything to base it on either way."

"What are you going to do about it?" Stan asked returning to his seat beside Maria.

Maria laughed. "That's Stan. We've defined the problem now let's get a solution. Let's not push her, Stan."

Katie held up her hand. "No, that's okay. My solution, so far, has been to try to put time, distance and other things in its place. I haven't been very successful. I thought if I ignored it, it would go away."

She paused thoughtfully. "Obviously that hasn't worked very well. Talking about, saying it out loud has helped." She smiled warmly at Stan and Maria. "Thanks for being my friends. I'm sorry I've been so rude to you this week. Will you forgive me?"

"On one condition," Stan said.

"What's that?"

"That you come to our Valentine's party next weekend."

"That sounds easy enough."

They talked some about the party and then discussed the new administration in Washington. It seemed that with a Republican controlled White House and Congress, some new initiatives were forthcoming to deal with the deficit and the sagging economy. While they didn't quite agree with the methods, they did agree to give them a chance before fully condemning them. It was an interesting discussion.

On her way home, Katie thought about the evening. Stan had a point about trying to handle tough situations all alone. Friends were important, more important than she had given thought to because she prided herself in her independence. But good friends like Stan and Maria were hard to come by. She had been so immersed in her own problems that she took them for granted, but not anymore. She would go to their party and she would have them over to her house and she would join the land of the living once again instead moving around the edges and hiding.

When she went to bed that night she fell asleep immediately and no unwanted pictures plagued her during the night. It was a good beginning.

9

Nine

Katie hurried and pulled her robe around her. She was in the middle of getting ready for the Valentine's party. The doorbell chimed again. Who could be calling? She wasn't expecting anyone. The bell sounded again. She hesitated a moment longer then went downstairs and looked through the peep hole. A strange man stood there with a bouquet of flowers in one hand. Behind him she could see a dark blue sports car. She turned her attention back to the man. He was of medium height and build. He had on a tan jacket with a plaid muffler tied around his neck, jeans and boots. The doorbell rang again. She looked to his face. She couldn't make out his features in the dim light.

"Who is it?" She asked.

"Steve Jackson."

Figures, she thought. What did he want? She opened the door and pulled the robe tighter around herself. He came in as she stepped back from the door. He surveyed her up and down and then smiled.

"I take it you weren't expecting me." He said.

"You are very observant. What are you doing here?"

"It's Valentine's Day and I thought you might enjoy a friendly face. Here." He handed her the flowers. "Happy Valentine's Day."

She took the flowers and smelled them trying to figure out what to say. He stood there obviously enjoying her speechlessness.

"You'd better not stand there all evening. We have a party to go to."

"Oh? We do? Where?" She asked sarcastically.

"The Colemans."

"Oh." She paused, feeling her cheeks begin to burn. "I guess I'd better get ready." She shoved the flowers back into his hands and hurried up the stairs.

She was embarrassed, mad, flattered, interested and nervous at the same time. The arrogance and confidence of the man waiting downstairs was unbelievable. If this was Stan's plan, he would hear from her, especially after their talk last week.

She was caught now, so she would go with this Steve Jackson to the party. She surveyed herself in the mirror. She had a long way to go. He could just wait.

Thirty minutes later she went back down stairs, a different woman. She had originally planned to wear jeans and a new sweater. But Steve Jackson's presence changed that. She went through her closet looking for something softer to wear. By the time she finished dressing she wasn't angry any more, instead a feeling of excitement and nervousness filled the center of her being. She felt confident of her appearance. She still wore jeans, but added a white cotton blouse with ruffles and a gray, gold, red, white and black scarf tied tightly around her waist. She curled her hair, and put on make-up.

As she neared the bottom of the stairs she could hear music coming from the living room. She glanced in the hall mirror and steadied her nerves. He was sitting on the couch, reading, Misty at his feet.

"Hi. I'm ready."

He looked up and she saw the approval in his eyes. "I guess it was worth the wait. You are beautiful."

"Thank you."

He stood and there was an awkward moment of silence as they stood looking at each other. He was cute. His face was square and strong. But the freckles that were spread across his nose and cheeks gave him a boyish look. His eyes were gray and his longish blond hair was tussled. Definitely cute, she thought.

"Well," she started moving to the hall, "we'd better get to the party. It's not fashionable to be late in Minnesota, and we are definitely late. We are going to the party, aren't we?" She had a moment of doubt. His nod reassured her.

"How well do you know Stan?" She asked, fishing to find out if this was a set up.

"Not too well," He said. "I met him this fall when I first moved here. We get together from time to time for lunch."

He paused. "Do you mind if I borrow this book? It's written by a friend of mine. I feel guilty because Chase Harrington was one of my best friends in law school and I knew he did a lot of writing, but I've never had or taken the time to read any of it. This one looks good. Is something wrong?"

She was momentarily stunned. How small could the world be anyway! A friend of Chase's, how ironic was that. Just when she was trying to forget him, she meets one of his best friends, great. But she didn't want him to know she knew Chase. "No, nothing's wrong." She replied smoothly. "I was just startled that you knew Chase Harrington. I use that book every semester in my Contemporary Affairs class. It's interesting you haven't read any of his things. I don't think there is anything of his I haven't read." She put on her cape and as she tied her scarf she turned to him. "You really haven't read anything of his?"

"No, I feel bad about it. But you know how time gets away from you. My work keeps me there twelve hours a day, six days a week. So many people need me and the services I provide. We are always understaffed and financed." He shrugged. "But that's a whole different story." He held up the book. "I'll read this though. Shall we get going?"

The drive to Stan's house was made in comfortable silence. They sat in the car for a couple of minutes and watched other people going into the house. Steve looked at her and grinned. "Did you say it wasn't fashionable to be late in Minnesota?" He waved his hand to indicate the other late comers. "It seems that there are many unfashionable people in this town." He regarded her for several minutes, his eyes never leaving hers. "You are quite beautiful, you know. I'm glad I took the risk of coming over. I figured the worst you could do was throw me out. I'm sorry if I upset you when I called last week. I didn't mean to. I guess I just didn't think. Am I forgiven?" He reached out to touch her. Then he leaned across the car to kiss her. She turned her head and his lips only brushed her cheek. He drew back. "You do forgive me, don't you?"

"Yes, I forgive you. I forgave you almost the second you hung up." She spoke lightly, trying to keep the trembling in her voice under control. This wasn't going very well. He was too confident and she wasn't sure of anything. "We'd better get inside," she continued. "I promised Stan and Maria I'd come and I know their little boys are waiting up to see me."

Steve followed her into the house where Stan greeted her with a kiss and a raised eyebrow. She whispered in his ear as she hugged him, "You set him up to this didn't you? Thanks a lot." She pulled back. "Sorry we're late. Are the boys still up?"

"Yes," Stan answered. "They're waiting for you. Maria's with them."

Katie quickly hurried up the stairs to the two waiting boys. "Aunt Katie, Aunt Katie," they yelled as she entered their room. "Look what we have for you." They jumped out of their beds and ran over to her, each holding a small heart shaped box. She bent down and hugged them. They were so cute. Maria came in the room and stood watching them. Katie went over to one of the beds and sat down with one boy on either side. She read their cards and opened the packages, two boxes of chocolates. She hugged the boys tightly. Over their heads her eyes met Maria's. Her eyes filled with tears. When she wiped her eyes the boys looked all concerned.

"Are you alright, Aunt Katie?"

"Oh, sure I am. I just want you both to know I love you very much." She kissed each one, "and thanks for the chocolates. I love chocolate." She stood. "Now it's time for bed."

This brought denials from them. But after a few minutes and with the help of Maria, they were tucked tightly in their beds.

Out in the hall, Maria stopped her. "Who is that guy that brought you tonight? You know you're going to have the town talking by morning."

"That man is Steve Jackson. I have a funny feeling your husband has something to do with this his being with me tonight. He called me a couple of weeks ago at Stan's suggestion. I didn't give him the time of day, in fact I was very rude. Well, tonight he came to the house while I was getting ready with a bouquet of flowers. And with the idea he was going to escort me here tonight. What could I do?" She shrugged.

Maria took her arm. "Stan hasn't said a word. He's very good looking. Is he nice?"

"Oh, he's Mr. Charming. He tried to make a pass at me in the car. I'm not real thrilled."

"But Katie, of course he tried to kiss you. Your beautiful

tonight and it is Valentine's Day, which makes it all so much more romantic. Be patient, promise?"

Katie looked into her pleading face and hesitated. "Okay, I promise to give him a chance." Wishing to get away from Maria's romantic notions, she said, "Come on, we'd better get back to the party."

As they came down the stairs, Katie could feel Steve's eyes on her. She felt very self-conscious. He was where she had left him, talking to Stan. When they reached them, she introduced Steve to Maria. She was right, Katie thought as she watched Steve; he was good-looking, and very sure of himself. She mentally added, be careful. He had thrown her for a loop when he said he was a close friend of Chase. It brought pictures back that she had spent the last two weeks blocking.

"Katherine."

She jumped.

Steve was speaking to her. "For the record, I want you all to hear this." He looked to Stan and Maria then back to her. "Stan did not put me up to surprising you and bringing you to the party tonight. It was my own idea. But I'm glad I did." He glanced at Stan and spoke as if she wasn't there. "She's much too interesting for me to ignore." His grey eyes had devils in them. "And I mean to provide some distraction from her determination to be constantly working."

Katie was embarrassed, her cheeks burning hot. She wasn't some object. He was much, too much, sure of himself. He needed to be put in his place. His grey eyes were mocking her, challenging her to do just that. He knew he had provoked her. He was waiting to see what she would do.

Well, she wasn't going to give him the satisfaction, especially in front of her best friends. Hearing music from the other room, she controlled herself and smiled sweetly at him, "I don't suppose you know how to dance?"

The devils were still in his eyes but he didn't say anything. The evening was going to be a battle of wills and she had to win. Steve was a charmer but his charm wasn't going to work on her.

She found out quickly that he knew how to dance. His step was sure and he led her firmly through difficult dances. She was a little uncomfortable being held so close. She became aware that other dancers were stopping to watch them. This made her even more uneasy. As if sensing her discomfort, he held her tighter and began leading her as if they were the only couple in the room. One by one, couples abandoned the floor in favor of watching them. She concentrated on following his steps. One, two, three, four, in, out, in, out, back around. It seemed like the music would never quit when all of a sudden there was clapping and she found herself self-consciously acknowledging it.

She looked to Steve and he was grinning broadly, the devils in his eyes dancing. Despite herself, she smiled. He had cleverly won and his pleasure at winning made him even more boyishly handsome. His charm was irresistible, but she would have to keep a check on it.

They left the now crowded dance floor in search of

breathing space. The dining room had been vacated in favor of the dance floor. The house wasn't a large one and Stan and Maria put most of the larger pieces from the living room into the dining room. This made the dining room cozier than normal. Through the double doors they could hear the laughter of the other guests.

She had held Steve's hand as they made their way out of the living room. She casually let go and walked over as if to examine the array of food on the table. She spied a punch bowl on one end and poured two glasses. Steve silently watched her and when she handed him his glass he motioned to one of the couches. She followed his direction and seated herself on one side. He followed suit, sitting at the opposite end.

She held her silence, sipping at her punch. She didn't play games or flirt. So she waited. The whole situation reminded her of the tension the day she learned that Chase Harrington was the name of the man who had rescued her from Mt. McLoughlin. She smiled as she remembered meeting Jake at the same time.

Steve caught her smile and smiled. "Why are you smiling? You weren't too ready to smile at me an hour ago."

She looked into his eyes and saw the devils dancing there. This guy was dangerous. "An hour ago you tried to make a pass at me. You don't even know me." She paused and softened the words with a smile. "But thank you for the dance." She said.

The devils left his eyes. "Come over here." He commanded quietly.

She looked searchingly into his eyes for a full minute then shook her head no.

A hundred different feelings went through her. She felt herself drawn to his charm. For some strange reason he reminded her of Chase. Perhaps it was because he had said he was an old friend of Chase's and also had that fresh, outdoors look. Except, he was very different from Chase. Chase was quiet, more reserved, he moved carefully through life, always conscious of the results of his actions. Steve, on the other hand, was bold and brash and confident. Through sheer will power, he would make things happen. He overwhelmed her.

She liked Steve Jackson. She couldn't deny that. But Chase was still a part of her, a part she couldn't easily get past. No matter how much she tried. The time she spent with Chase seemed like a dream, but the ache inside was real. The thought of ever being with him again was a dream beyond her imagination. She wished she knew where he fit in, if there was a place for him in her future.

"Hey," Steve said softly. "What's the matter?"

"Nothing." She looked into his grey eyes and noticed in surprise they had gold flecks in them. She pushed the conflicting thoughts away and concentrated on Steve. Why, she wondered, did he bring me to the party? He could have met her here. It was on the tip of her tongue to ask, but she held back. She didn't want to know the answer. Not yet.

"Where are you from?" She asked, feeling safe.

"Tacoma, Washington." He answered. "How about you?"

They settled into talking about general things, getting to know each other. He seemed to be okay with being the one doing most of the talking.

It was while they were talking that Maria found them. "Oh, there you are. I wondered where you disappeared to." Her dark eyes twinkled as if the three of them held a secret together. "I hope you are enjoying yourselves, I know there are a lot of students here."

"It's a lovely party." Katie assured Maria, with a smile.

"Well you took the place by storm with your dancing. I didn't know you could dance like that, Katie."

"Oh," She protested. "I'm not a good dancer. Steve led. I just followed."

"Well, whatever." Maria smiled. "Now I want you two out of here. None of the kids will come in because they're afraid of interrupting you. I think Stan's going to play some slow songs, if you'd like to dance again."

Steve looked at Katie and she shrugged, "Why not? Maria wants us to mingle anyway."

The lights were turned down in the living room. She saw Stan over by the stereo controlling the mood. "Excuse me." She said to Steve. Stan watched her come across the room with a small smile on his face.

"Enjoying yourself?" He asked.

"Yes, surprisingly I am."

"Thanks a lot!"

"No, I didn't mean…"

He placed his hand on her arm and his eyes were warm. "I know what you mean." He looked over to where Steve was watching the dancers. "You two seemed to have hit it off."

"I suppose so."

"Good."

"I don't know." She followed his eyes and smiled to herself. He caught the smile. He spoke and she turned her attention back to him.

"I've involved myself enough in your private life, so I'll stay out now, but I hope you remember what we talked about last week. If you need anything. Anything. You know where to find us."

She regarded her friend thoughtfully for a moment. "You can count on it. Thank you."

She made her way back to Steve. He smiled and opened his arms in an invitation. She stepped to him and they began to move to the music. Steve held her closely to him. Couples moved around them. Songs changed. She was only aware of the man holding her. He held her right hand tightly to his chest and she could feel his other hand lying casually around her waist. Her other arm was curled around his neck and she laid her head against his shoulder.

He broke the silence. "What did you say to Stan?"

"I just told him I was enjoying the party."

"Are you?"

She lifted her head to look at him. "Yes. Are you?"

He leaned forward and kissed her lightly. "Does that answer your question?"

"No. Not really."

The devils were alive and dancing. "You're not the trusting sort, are you?"

She smiled at him. "No. I'm not. Trust is built through honesty and consistency..." She paused. "You're laughing at me, aren't you?" She backed off and moved her arm to his shoulder.

"Don't get angry. You're too idealistic; you scare men away. Lucky for you, I don't scare easily."

"Really? I think you're crazy." She tried to relax and let the music take her mind away.

They went for a drive after leaving the party. Steve followed the road that led to the top of the bluffs which surrounded the river valley, where the town of St. Peter lay, sleeping. They had the road and the view to themselves.

There was a full moon and everything lay white and glimmering in its light, as if someone had spilled a bunch of silver sequins over the earth. They drove in silence. Each lost in their own thoughts.

There was a scenic overview along this road and Steve pulled into it. The view was magnificent as the valley lay silent and blinking under the night sky. Steve opened her door and they went to the edge, arm in arm.

"Beautiful, isn't it?" He asked.

"Yes, it is. This is one of my favorite views in the area. I almost think I am in the mountains when I'm here."

"You like the mountains, don't you?" He turned to her.

"Yes. How do you know?" She asked, puzzled.

"I could hear the longing in your voice."

"Oh." Was I that easy to read, she wondered? Suddenly she felt very tired. She looked up into Steve's face. Even though it was dark, she could see the gold flecks. He leaned forward and kissed her, lightly, exploring. His arms tightened around her as his lips left hers and made a trail across her face to her neck, then back to her lips before he lifted his head. "Want to come home with me?" He asked his voice husky.

"No." She said softly. "I don't think so."

He was silent a moment. "I suppose you're right." He said quietly.

They stood silent, waiting, looking for signs in each other's eyes. He smiled. The tension broke. "Okay, I'll take you home. But I'll call again."

10

Ten

The next afternoon the telephone rang. Katie looked up with a start, annoyed at the intrusion. It rang again. She hurried to answer it, leaving her desk strewn with paper.

"Hello."

"Hello, Katie?" It was Steve.

"Yes. Hello Steve." She sat down in a nearby chair. He was right about calling again, she didn't expect it would be so soon.

"How are you today?"

"I'm tired from too much dancing last night."

"What are you doing now? Mind if I stop over for a while?"

"I don't know, Steve. I'm trying to get some writing done and it's not going very well. Plus, I've got a mound of papers to read and grade."

"It'll only be for a while. I'd like to see you."

She hesitated. "Okay."

"Great. I'll be over in a few minutes."

"See you soon."

Katie hung up the phone slowly. Then she poured another cup of coffee. On her way back to the study she stopped to survey herself in the mirror. She looked horrible. She was tired and it showed. It was late when Steve brought her home. She didn't sleep well and was awake early. She had a headache and felt like she had slept too much. She took a drink of the coffee and studied herself closer. She had on old blue jeans with patches on both knees, an old red flannel shirt with long underwear underneath for warmth. Her hair was disheveled and her eyes were dark and tired. Her energy was at its lowest ebb. She shrugged. She didn't care.

She sat at her desk and stared at the paper before her. During the night an idea of a poem came to her and she had spent the morning and a good part of the afternoon trying to get it out. Now that the basic idea was written down she needed to smooth out the rough edges.

It was about the dilemma she was struggling with inside, the one that had begun last night. She laid her head in her arms. Where did Chase fit in? Did he fit in? She sat up and pushed her hair back again. And now Steve was coming over to see her.

The doorbell rang and she heard the door open. "Katie?" Steve came into the hallway.

Without rising she called, "In here."

He came into the small study and looked around him

curiously. The desk at which she sat was placed in front of the only window, there was a comfortable old chair in one corner with a reading lamp hanging over it, a sewing area and machine lined another wall and the remaining wall contained floor to ceiling bookshelves filled with books, fabric and baskets.

"This is where you escape with the musty ideas of dead men." He said.

"It is also a room full of live ideas. Mine." She didn't stand up.

"You look awful, you know. What'd you do, stay out all night with some crazy guy?"

She could see the devils dancing in his eyes. "You're right on one count, the part about the crazy guy." She relaxed a bit and gave him a warm smile, then sobered. "I'm tired." She looked out her window, for a moment lost to the present. She caught herself and turned back to face him, lightly asking, "And how are you today? You seem to be well rested and relaxed."

"I am. I slept great." He went over to the desk and picked up the poem she had been working on. She didn't make any effort to stop him. She moved and sat in the old chair in the corner. He looked at her, "Is this what you were working on?"

She nodded.

"May I?"

She nodded again. Her stomach tightened up. She watched his face as he read. She couldn't tell what he was thinking.

He sat down at the desk and reread it. Finally, he looked back over to her.

"It's beautiful."

"Thank you."

"Who are you in love with?"

"I don't know. It's not necessarily about who I am in love with, it's about love."

"What?"

Katie drew in a deep breath. How much should she tell him? After all he was a part of the turmoil. "Well," she hesitated again. She looked over to him, his gaze catching hers and holding it. She could see the questions in his eyes. She tore her eyes away and looked at her hands. She got up and began to aimlessly walk around the room. She looked at him again. Feeling a little surer of herself, but not any calmer she sat down and began. "What I mean is." She stopped. This was not going to be easy. How could she tell him she was in love with his best friend from law school? She couldn't. That was that. But she felt she had to answer him, since she let him read the poem.

Steve was reading the poem again. He looked up. "I'm in here, aren't I?"

"Yes."

"Which one am I?"

"It's not about which one."

"How can you say that?" He asked incredulously.

"Because I wrote it." She stood by the desk, starring out the window, and then faced him. "I shouldn't have let you read it."

He pulled her against him. "I'm sorry, Katie. You don't have to tell me."

She looked up at him and pushed herself away. "Yes, I do have to tell you. You're in that poem. You're a part of it." She paused to steady her voice. She took a deep breath and plunged ahead. "Last fall I went backpacking with my brother and his friends in Oregon. We climbed a mountain and I got sick at the peak and went back down to camp by myself. Only I was too foolish to acknowledge I was sick and I never made it down. I twisted my ankle and fell into a gully. I was almost dead from the fall and exposure. I was found there, rescued, really, by a man who lives in the mountains there. He took care of me, got me on my feet and helped me get back home. I think I fell in love with him. I didn't know it at the time."

"How could you not know you fell in love? Where is he now?"

"I don't know you that well," she said. "But not everyone is as sure of themselves as you seem to be."

He didn't seem to know what to say to that.

"I had a good time last night. I will admit I am attracted to you, but beyond that I can't say."

He was silent a few moments and ran his fingers through his already tousled hair. "I suppose that will have to do," he said. "You're the most interesting person I have met in the few months I have lived here, so I'm not going to go away."

Steve wanted to stay longer, but she made him leave. She needed to be alone. She sat at her desk and studied the poem. Where was she? Where did she fit in?

She pushed herself away from the desk and wandered into the kitchen. She poured herself another cup of coffee and sat at the kitchen table, staring out the window. The sun was just setting and the snow banks reflected the rosy glow of the western sky.

It had been a beautiful day. The sky had been clear blue, bringing everything into sharper focus. It was the kind of day that usually sent her spirits soaring. But not today. There was too much weighing on her mind.

She went over the details of the previous evening again. Steve Jackson was a different sort of guy. He was so confident in himself and the impression he made on others. That powerful confidence set her back a couple of paces, but in the course of the evening she learned he was made of much softer stuff. She was attracted to him. He interested her, but she wasn't sure how much.

She thought of Chase. He was everything she thought she wanted in a man; intelligent, caring, independent. He was stronger than her. She was a strong woman, she knew that. She could take care of herself. But she was tired of taking care of herself, so tired of it.

It was all such a dream. She wanted Chase, not Steve. But Chase was beyond her. Steve was here. He was real. Could Steve dominate her dreams? He would try. She smiled at the thought.

She got up from the table and went into the living room. She sat down on the couch. Misty ran over to her from her corner where she had been sleeping. She reached down and pulled her into her lap. Why did she let herself get caught up in mind games? It never solved anything.

“Can you tell me, Misty?” She asked.

Finding no answer, she returned to her desk and began to grade papers.

Later that evening she was still at her desk when the telephone rang.

“Are you okay?” Steve asked without preamble.

“Yes, I am thank you.” She said. “Sorry about this afternoon, I don’t usually fall apart.”

“Good. You sound better.” He paused. “Katie, I know we’ve only just met, but I meant what I said, and I’m not going away. I’ll be here if you need me.”

“Thanks. I’ll remember that.” She said dryly.

“You don’t believe me.” It was a statement.

“As you said, we only just met.”

He was silent. She waited. He was silent a few moments longer.

“Dinner tomorrow night? I’ll pick you up from school at 5:30. Wear something pretty.” He hung up the phone before she got a chance to reply.

She put the phone thoughtfully back on the hook. Chase may be her dream, but Steve was real, real, and, she stopped. No more analyzing. Just take it for what it was, she told herself. Let things and time take its course.

11

Chapter Eleven

Sunrise

glistens on dew-drenched grass;

whose wetness kisses night gone.

And I will look unto the mountains,

from whence shall my help come?

The May breeze blew through Katie's hair as she worked among the new shoots of her garden. The sun felt good upon her back after the long months of winter chill. Spring was a time of beginning and she was looking forward to the coming months. The winter had been very hard. There were times when she thought she had lost her ability to reason and sort reality from hopeful dreams. Many times she thought she had won the battle of mind games, when suddenly they would start up again. The uncertainty of her emotions sapped her self-confidence.

It was good to be out of the confines of her house and working with her hands. It helped relieve the burden of time and thoughts that crept up on her during the harsh months of winter. School was almost over, only finals remained, and as she only tested two of her four classes, the bulk of her work was finished. The semester had passed in a blur. Katie was not at her best. There were too many sleepless nights filled with questions.

Perhaps she didn't fail her students; they continued to stop by her office to talk. Student, teacher interaction was important to Katie. She didn't particularly care if students remembered when Napoleon took over France, when D Day was, or when the Civil War ended. If they were stimulated to think, wonder and seek answers to questions that had remained unanswered throughout time she was satisfied. No, I guess I didn't fail them, she thought, only myself. Ashamed she let emotional conflicts destroy so much valuable time.

She stood up from her work to stretch. She had finished weeding over half the garden. She was satisfied. She looked at her watch, 4 pm. Where did the time go? Picking up her tools she walked to the house. Misty was curled up sleeping in the sun by the steps. She let her be and went inside. She had a lot to do before Steve came over. The kitchen was a mess. She was a mess. She had to get the picnic dinner ready. He was due at 6 pm.

Two hours later, Katie sat down to wait for the chicken to finish baking. She had cleaned the kitchen, taken a shower and put on clean clothes. The salad, rolls, wine, and everything else they needed was in the picnic basket. Steve was due at any moment. She didn't feel too relaxed.

She drew a deep breath. It was beautiful out! Spring was her second favorite season, next to fall of course. She liked the way everything came to life and the freshness of the colors. Fall was glorious in a different way. The colors were as exuberant, and they too were in celebration of life, only it wasn't fresh life, if was life before death. It was the last chance to enjoy nature before it all faded away in the cold darkness of winter.

Katie felt two hands on her shoulders. She started. Steve!

"I caught you sleeping." He eyed her mischievously. "Tired already? You're going to be a lot of fun."

She regarded him with a look that was meant to be serious, but she couldn't help smiling. "I wasn't sleeping, I was thinking."

"Right, then why were your eyes closed and why didn't you hear me when I came in?"

"Alright, you win! I was sleeping."

"As usual." He pulled her out of the chair into his arms. "You're an interesting woman, Katie. You pretend you're your own woman and like I'm not needed. You fight me. But secretly, you need me, only you don't want me to know. You know what? You don't fool me anymore."

Katie listened to him patiently. And when he bent his head to kiss her, she met him half way. She had heard this all before. She was self-sufficient and independent, but she was tired of being alone. Her independence had cost her so much already.

She finished getting dinner together while Steve played with Misty in the yard. She watched them thoughtfully for a minute before going out. Steve was a wonderful man, and their relationship was growing stronger. She depended on him. She wanted to depend on him as much as he wanted her to depend on him. And he knew it. She smiled. He was so sure of himself. He knew what he wanted and he was going to get it. She shrugged and went outside to put things into the car while Steve put Misty into her kennel.

They got in the car and drove with the windows down. Katie stuck her head out to feel the wind blow through her hair, and then she pulled back inside to smile at Steve. "Isn't this a gorgeous day? So, what did you do all day?"

"Thought about you."

"That must have been exciting."

"It was."

His tone of voice chased the light banter from her lips. She studied his face a moment then stuck her head out the window again, letting the force of the wind hit her face full on. Something was going on inside the head of the man across the seat from her and she wondered what exactly he had been thinking about all day.

She pulled back inside, looking at Steve. He caught her eye and smiled. They drove on in pleasant silence enjoying the end of a spring day in May. The trees were pretty, dark and bare from a distance, but up close you could see the green shoots bursting out of the small buds. The undergrowth was beginning to show signs of life. Little flecks of purple and white against the fresh green gave evidence of the wild flowers. Yes, Katie thought, it was a beautiful day.

The park they chose for their evening picnic was situated on one of the bluffs along the Minnesota River and gave a commanding view of the valley. They walked on a trail along the ridge looking for a grassy spot in which to spread their fare.

In ten minutes, they found the spot for which they had been looking, a small patch of grass sheltered with shrubbery yet open to the view of the river valley. The golden hour was upon them, one of the best times of the day.

"This is perfect." Katie put down the basket and moved to take in the full view. Steve came up behind and put his arms around her.

"Isn't this a beautiful view?" Katie asked.

"Look," Steve pointed to the north. "There's your house."

She followed his outstretched hand and could barely make out the features which made the dot in the valley hers. There were large trees in the front yard. She could see the dog house, garden and fruit trees in the back yard, where the grove took up residence and left off at the neighbor's cornfield.

"Look, you can see where the corn is just coming up."

"Where?" He peered into the gathering dusk.

"See the thin thread of green going through the field

behind my grove?" She pointed towards it. "You have to look really hard."

He looked again for several moments. "Oh, I see it. There?" He indicated. "You'd need binoculars to see that."

"You just have to know what you're looking for in order to see it."

They were silent for a few minutes just taking in the scene.

"Well, I know what I'm looking for." He said.

"Oh? What's that?" She leaned back to look at him, thinking he meant something in the valley below.

"Someone like you."

She looked at him a moment, then turned back to the view. It would be dusk soon as the sun began its descent to below the horizon; leaving in its wake a rose, violet, azure and yellow glow across the horizon.

She moved out of the circle of his arms to where they dropped their things. Steve quietly lit the kerosene lantern they had brought while Katie opened the picnic basket. He set the lantern off to the side where its soft glow gently shed light over their picnic without chasing the shadows. The air was cooler so she put on her sweater.

She looked around feeling pleasantly relaxed. Her eyes stopped at Steve. Standing there in his jeans and polo shirt with wind swept hair reminded her of the first time she met him. He caught her grin.

"What's so funny?" He asked.

"I was remembering the first time I met you."

"That's funny?"

"Think about it. You came over to take me to a party on Valentine's Day without asking me, because you knew I'd turn you down cold if you'd have asked me. And you brought flowers. What girl would turn a man away on Valentine's Day if he had flowers?"

"Yeah, I guess it is funny when you look back on it. I was scared you'd throw me out flat on my face."

"I was tempted, believe me. But I was intrigued and decided to take a risk, not, as you know, something I normally do."

"Intrigued? Interesting. Has the risk been worth it?" His voice had lost its teasing note.

Katie thought about it while she brought the food out. He was fishing for something. He was acting a little strange, a little uncertain. She gave him his glass and poured the wine. Then she filled her glass. "Help yourself." She handed him the chicken.

He regarded her with his blue eyes. "You haven't answered my question."

"I'm thinking about it." She was treading on uncertain ground here. She took some chicken and salad before going on. "Well," still she hesitated, thinking. "Yes, I am glad I took the risk. You are a lot of fun."

"A lot of fun?" He asked. "I didn't think of it like that. I suppose you are right. We do have a lot of fun together. You constantly amaze me and I enjoy it – you- very much. As I told you at the beginning, you're the most interesting person I know here."

"Well," she said. "I'm glad you find me interesting. You're fun, I'm interesting." She paused, not looking at him, time to find out what was going on. "What's on your mind anyway?" She asked.

"You."

"Be serious."

"I am."

She looked up at him thoughtfully. He kept eating, then noticed her and smiled. His seriousness of moments ago was gone. It was as if he had gone backstage and put on a mask. He could change faces, moods, in an instant. She didn't feel she really knew him. It bothered her sometimes. She didn't completely trust him but she wasn't sure she was really ready to trust anyone yet. Not in the way that counted.

The food was gone. Together they put everything back into the basket. "More wine?" Steve asked leaning forward.

"Just a bit." The day's work, good food, and good company worked as a balm, soothing the tension of the previous moment.

Steve lifted his glass in a toast. "To you."

Katie hesitated, and then lifted hers, "To us."

They touched glasses and finished the wine in silence. Steve was weighing his next words, she could tell. The mask was off and his blue eyes were intense. He took her wine glass and put it away with his. He seemed to pause at the end of his task. Yet, she was reluctant to say he hesitated because it was so unlike him. He never hesitated. She felt something begin to form in her stomach. She tried to ignore it.

When he came to her, she let him take her face in his hands. His kiss was long and soft. It was nice, but that was it. Then he turned out the lantern and they were alone with the stars. She looked up and without reason and for only a moment was back in Oregon. But it was long enough. She felt her eyes mist over.

Steve took her hand in his, misreading her face he said, "The stars are so beautiful, aren't they? Every night they're there. You can count on them. Just think of it. All through the ages, what they've seen. It's amazing."

"It is incredible." She looked at him, then back skyward. "I always think of God when I look at the stars. That He's there looking over His world. I wonder at His creation and I see His glory in the stars. Do you see?"

They both looked skyward for a few minutes. She could feel God's strength reaching to her. It was miraculous. Steve seemed to catch her feeling. "Yes." He said slowly. "I can see what you mean." He paused. "You are remarkable. You see things that would never occur to me."

They were back to earth again. She felt his arms tighten around her. Then he kissed her hair, her ears, neck before resting his chin on her.

"Did I tell you I love you?"

She didn't answer.

He pulled back and even in the dim light, she could see the gold flecks in his eyes. "I love you. Katherine."

He waited. But the words he wanted to hear were stuck in her throat. At the disappointment in his eyes, she slid out of his embrace. At the edge of the bluff she stood, listening to the night sounds. The cricket's chorus was loud and echoed out over the valley. The call of the morning dove was heard in the distance. She watched without seeing the evening traffic on the highway below. The knot in her stomach was tightening.

After a while she became aware of his presence beside her. She turned away from the valley. Uncertainly she held his eyes a moment. Steve held out his arms, his eyes willing her to come to him. She resisted. He dropped his arms. She hesitated. He waited.

Katie spoke slowly, "I'm sorry, but I can't say the words you long to hear from me. I care about you very much, I don't know why but they won't come. Can you understand that?"

He remained silent. He was used to getting what he wanted.

"You are very important to me," she plunged ahead. "It's too fast."

"Why don't you trust me? Why can't you take a risk and trust me?"

"I did take a risk." She protested. "I'm here with you. I've been with you all winter. I need you Steve, can't you see that?"

In response he pulled her close. She laid her head against him as he smoothed her hair. She was shaking. She couldn't lose him. Not when she was just beginning to forget Chase. Chase. His face flashed for an instant before her eyes. She couldn't lose them both to the memory of time. She just needed more time.

"It's alright, Katie." He whispered against her. "Let's go home."

Later when he left her at her doorstep he said, "Katie, I love you. I'm sorry if that scares you, but I do. I know now that you're not ready. I will wait for you. But I can't wait forever."

When he kissed her good night, it was a tender kiss. But she could feel his longing. And as other times, his kiss didn't stir anything inside of her.

His warning rang in her ears long after she turned off the light.

#

She saw the earth come rushing up to her. She put out her hands . . .

Katie woke up shaking and sweating. It was the same dream she had in Oregon. Chase had been there last time when she had awakened. She remembered she didn't want him to be near her. But she had completely forgotten, until now, how he had held her until she was quietly sleeping again.

She reached out and turned on the bedside light, fingers shaking slightly. She shook her head, trying to dispel the shadows chasing each other. Pulling her knees to her chin she longed so much for Chase it was a physical ache. His face flashed before her closed eyes — tousled, tired, and tender. His eyes stayed even after the other features had fled by. Deep and dark, she saw in them tenderness she'd never seen before or since. Not even in Steve's eyes.

She felt as though she had been struck by lightning. Chase loved her. She felt it with a certainty that made her heart pound. She turned off the light and embraced the memories until sleep finally overtook them.

The first rays of light woke her. She sat up feeling bewildered. Then remembering the night's revelations, she got up and went outside. The sun wasn't quite up, but the earth already knew of its presence below the eastern horizon. It wouldn't be long and day would be upon them in all its splintered glory.

She stretched, loosening her sleep cramped legs. She woke Misty. And as the sun poked its head over the horizon, she began to run.

She turned out onto the deserted road. She concentrated on lifting her feet and holding her body straight as though she was pushing a wall with her hands. Eventually her body got the rhythm and she could free her mind.

It was a still, clear morning. Only the birds were beginning to stir. She could hear their music as they sought to get in tune with the day. She felt as if she could run forever. All the hope she had entertained of ever forgetting Chase, to live her life peacefully and contently without him, was gone. It vanished in the dark. She pulled in a deep breath, as if air alone would give her peace of mind.

It angered her that a dream could touch her so deeply. She concentrated on running, banishing other thoughts from her head. Left, right; left, right; up, down; up, down; hold your body straight; relax your upper body; channel your energy. For what?

The dam opened again. She continued to run. Memories poured through. She let them flow over the contours of her brain, into her blood. She picked up her pace. Chase, Chase, Chase pounded with every step.

She turned a corner and slowed her pace to fit the terrain. By the time she reached the top of the bluff all the memories of Oregon had passed through her. She remembered every detail, every touch, every word, every look, as though it was just yesterday. And she knew, as she did last night, that he did, indeed, love her. Her illness and weak condition blinded her to that fact. She felt vulnerable and scared. She always thought, even after she knew she loved him, that he hadn't given her any particular indication that he loved her. But now she knew. She just did.

She reached the top and paused to look out over the valley. The sun was midway to the point where it slowed to give light all day.

What triggered all these memories? Why now? Why now after all this time? Why this certainty, based on memories? Why was she so sure, down at the bottom of her pile of faith, that Chase loved her? Where would this knowledge take her? How many corners would she have to turn before coming face to face with him again? And did she have enough faith to hope?

She turned and began the ascent back into the valley.

And more importantly, she thought, what of Steve and his declaration and warning? What was she to do with him in light of her new-found conviction? Deny him on the faith of her hope?

She reached the driveway to her house with no answers. She needed to get away.

12

Twelve

The dogs raced up to greet Katie when she pulled into the farmyard two hours later. She got out of the car and looked around. The lawn had been mowed, the garden just planted. She looked beyond the cattle yard to the pasture. The cattle were out grazing, tiny dots of brown on the green hillside.

She drew in a deep breath to steady her nerves. It smelled like a farm. It was good to be home.

She walked up to the house. The dogs hadn't barked so no one inside knew she was there.

"Hello. I'm home." She called as she entered the shadows of the house.

"Katie, is that you?" She heard mom's voice before she came out of her room in her half-dressed Sunday morning attire. She opened her arms and held Katie in a welcoming warm hug.

She ate a breakfast roll and fresh egg while her parents finished dressing for church.

"What brings you home, Katie?" Alex Carlson asked later as they drove to church.

"I needed to get away."

"How long will you be staying?"

"Just till tomorrow morning. I have to give a final at eleven. So I'll leave after breakfast. If that's okay? I should have called, but I just decided this morning to come, so..."

"You know it is. We like to see you once in a while!"

They arrived at church. John was already sitting in the sanctuary so they slipped in beside him. He looked at Katie in surprise. "What are you doing home?"

"I had to get away."

"How long are you home for?"

"Just today."

The welcome and announcements were over. It was time for the opening song. It was good to be in the church of her childhood and youth. Familiar loving faces were on all sides. There were memories in each one.

Katie found comfort in the service. Her thoughts were quieted and she was filled with peace. God works in mysterious ways. She had always been taught that. She also knew that each person would have to discover this for themselves. Katie knew that she was moving in a direction she absolutely had no control over. Being here today reminded her that as long as she had faith, she had direction. It was a reminder she had desperately needed.

Alex and Martha Carlson had already decided to try out a new restaurant in town, so they agreed to meet there for Sunday dinner. Katie went with John.

"So, this isn't like you," John said. "What's up? Does it have to do with Steve?"

"Yes. I needed to get away, get some space. He's been pushing me hard to make a commitment I'm not ready to make."

"Because of last fall?"

"Yes, in part. On the one hand I want to be in a relationship, for companionship and friendship. On the other it feels forced."

"I'm not one with a lot of good relationship advice. But I will say this, you keep listening to what your gut says, not what he says, or anyone else. It's your life."

"Thanks John, that's great advice."

They drove in companionable silence to the restaurant as Katie felt some of the tension dissipate.

"How have you been?" Martha Carlson asked her daughter after they were seated and placed their orders. She reached out to wipe a strand of hair out of Katie's eyes. "You look tired. Have you been working too hard?"

"Yes. As the semester winds down, there is that final push to the end. You know, papers to grade, finals to write, give and grade. But I'm in pretty good shape." She took in a breath. She was so tired, her eyes felt like hollows inside her head. "I had a nightmare last night. A really bad one. I had trouble sleeping and I was awake early. So, I decided I needed a change of scenery."

Martha reached out and squeezed her hand. "You're always welcome here. It's good to see you."

Their eyes held a moment in the unspoken understanding that only mothers and daughters can know. It was comforting, but she had wanted to talk to them and get their advice. After her conversation with John, she wasn't so sure anymore.

Alex unknowingly opened the door to the topic of Steve anyway.

"So, Katie," he said. "When are we going to meet this Steve we've heard so much about?"

Katie hesitated a moment. Now that they asked she didn't know where to start.

"Katie?" Martha asked concern in her eyes as well as her voice. "Is everything okay?"

She shook her head. "No, it's not okay and I don't know why. Well, I do, but it is really confusing."

"What do you mean?" Martha prompted.

She took a deep breath. "Well, everything was going good. You know we were having fun together and stuff, not too serious, but good. Then last night," she paused, not sure how much she wanted to reveal. "Well, let's just say he would like to get serious."

"I see." Martha said.

"Is that a problem?" Alex asked.

"Yes." She was growing tense again. She briefly closed

her eyes and absently pushed her hair back. She could feel her stomach playing games again and fought it. "I just don't know." She mumbled. Trying to put into words what she was feeling, but failing.

"What did you say?" Martha asked.

"Nothing." She looked at the three of them. They waited. "I care about Steve a lot. He's a great guy, smart, funny, caring, cute. But I'm not in love, not hopelessly, passionately in love." She paused. "You know what I mean."

"Love isn't always that way," Alex said.

"I know." She said. "But you have to feel right about it. I think there should be something more. He's like my best friend right now, period."

"He's not asking you to decide right away is he?" Martha asked.

"No. But he will soon. He's not satisfied with being a friend. He plays for keeps. And now the gauntlet has been laid. He's waiting." She shrugged, hearing again his words of warning as he left her last night.

John sat listening quietly. Katie could tell he was wondering about Chase. He was the only one who had met Chase and knew about him.

"Well, honey," Alex said. "You don't have to decide today. So just relax and forget about everything in St. Peter until tomorrow."

"Everything but the papers I brought with to grade." Katie smiled. She felt the tension melt away and again was thankful she had come home.

When they returned to the farm, Katie went up to her old room and changed into jeans and a t-shirt. She went down to the kitchen to work on papers. Martha and Alex's bedroom door was closed, time for a Sunday afternoon nap.

Katie worked for about an hour. But she couldn't concentrate. So she went upstairs and fell asleep as soon as her head hit the pillow.

Sometime later, she felt the bed sag beside her. She opened her eyes. "Hi Mom. What time is it?"

"Five. Dad is out doing chores. You've been asleep since 3. I thought I'd better wake you so you'll be able to sleep tonight."

Katie remained silent, not wishing to disturb the drowsiness that enveloped her. She felt so relaxed. "Mom?"

"Hmm?"

"What do you do when you love somebody and you know he loves you too but you don't know if you'll ever see him again?"

"You're not talking about Steve." It was a statement.

"No." She thought for a few minutes. "It was when I had the accident in Oregon. It is the man who found me." She went on to tell her the whole story from when she first became aware of Chase to the dream last night. "I don't know what to do." She concluded. "I care about Steve and don't want to lose his friendship. At the same time, I love Chase and I think he loves me. But I'm afraid to hope I'll ever see him again."

"I suspected something like this," she answered. "I can

see why you're confused. The situation in Oregon had to have been pretty emotionally charged. You were obviously attracted to him. I don't have an answer. But I wonder why he didn't try to contact you?"

"I wondered about that too. A lot. But he only knew my name and that I was from Minnesota."

"Well," she said. "I think you're going to have to keep doing what you've been doing. Wait and see. What do you do about Steve? That's up to you. But you need to be careful when you're playing with a man's heart."

"Yea." Katie could see again the disappointment in Steve's eyes. "I know you're right. I don't know what I'll do, but it sure has helped to finally talk about it. Thanks, mom."

"That's what moms are for," Martha said as she wrapped her arms around her daughter. "I love you Katie."

#

After a light supper, Martha and Alex left for church, choir practice and the evening service. Katie stayed home to continue working on grading papers. Almost as soon as they were down the driveway, however, she abandoned them and went for a walk. The corn was just beginning to come up in the field south of the driveway. The cattle were in the yard eating grain and quenching their thirst in the tank. Katie took the field road around the grove that led to the fields east of the farmstead, to the old gravel pit and cow pasture. She could smell farm in the air, the animals and the freshness of spring.

She reached the top of the highest hill in the pasture. From here she could see everywhere. She sat down in the tall grass to watch the sun set. For the third time that day, scenes from her stay with Chase went through her mind. She savored them, knowing she couldn't allow herself the pleasure again for some time.

John found her there.

"Hi John!" Katie said. "What are you doing here?"

He had purposefully waited until he knew Alex and Martha had left before he came over. He had held his silence during lunch, but he was concerned about her. Ever since she had come back from Oregon, she just wasn't herself. It was time to have a talk.

"I wanted to see how you were, really." He said as he sat down beside her in the tall grass.

She really didn't want to talk about it, again. "Just what I said this noon. Steve wants more from me than I am ready to give right now."

"What about Chase?"

She gave him a startled look. She had never said a word to him about Chase.

"Look," he said, "I was there. I was in the hospital room with you. He nearly bit my head off because I let you go down Mt. McLoughlin alone. I'm not stupid. There was something more going on there between you."

"I know. But I don't know what. And we never talked about it and he hasn't tried to find me and," she paused as she watched the sun slip quietly over the horizon. "I don't owe him anything."

"What about what you owe yourself? You can't go on this way. It's been almost a year. Something needs to change. Think about it." He stood and reached out a hand to her in the fading daylight.

"Okay," was all she could say, his words bringing her back to the reality of her situation. Once again she resolved to pursue her day to day life, to wait without waiting. She had to go back to school in the morning. She had a relationship with Steve that while she didn't want to get serious, she didn't want to break it off yet. Right now she wanted to have the best of both worlds.

Katie loved Chase. She believed he loved her too. She just wasn't sure what she wanted to do about it, or could do about it. But maybe John was right; she owed it to herself to find out.

Maybe she just didn't have the faith to hope. But yet, she did. She tucked that hope into a tiny compartment in her heart.

13

Thirteen

Katie picked up the last of the exam papers. Finals were over for the year. She felt a sense of relief even though she had stacks of tests waiting to be graded. But when those were done, she had freedom for three months.

She checked around the room to make sure she hadn't left anything. Then she went back to her little office to attack the pile of tests. First, she poured herself a cup of coffee.

It was the end of a long week. She had returned to school on Monday, refreshed, in time to administer the first exam. When the testing period was over, she spent the rest of the day grading papers. At six her telephone rang. "Hello."

"Katie, where have you been?" It was Steve.

"Hi Steve," She put down her pen, tucked the phone under her ear while she poured a cup of coffee.

"Katie, where did you disappear to yesterday?"

"I went home for the day and came back this morning."

"At least you could have told me. I tried calling you all morning Sunday. Finally, I drove over and found the place all locked up. I couldn't figure out where you went."

"Listen, Steve." She was tired and just a bit annoyed. "I've been reading and trying to grade these papers all afternoon. I've got a lot to get finished here. I needed a break yesterday and so I went home to visit my parents. I didn't realize I needed to tell you first."

"Okay. Sorry to bother you." Click. He hung up.

That was Monday today was Friday. A whole week had passed and he hadn't called her. She didn't call him either. She needed some time to be alone. She had a lot of thoughts to sort through regarding their relationship, especially where she stood with him. But she realized today she missed him.

She pushed thoughts of Steve away and turned her attention to the papers and tests of her students. A couple hours later she put the exam papers away. Although she had made a sizeable dent in the pile she had quite a bit left to do. She put the remainder into her brief case to take home. The sooner she finished grading tests the sooner she would be free for the summer.

Although Katie's summer plans weren't complete, she had made a long list of things to do. The first was to finish a book of poems and get them to New York. This time she would go personally and renew her acquaintance with the city. Second, she wanted to re-familiarize herself with the period of history surrounding World Wars I and II. That in itself was a huge task, but it would make her teaching fresh. The third thing she wanted to do was review several books and do some sewing projects. Those things were in addition to her regular summer projects such as gardening and canning.

She intentionally did not include spending time with Steve on her to do list. She simply did not know more than the fact she had fun with him and appreciated his company. She didn't believe for a second that would be enough for him.

As she drove home through the gathering twilight, she realized a part of her was dreading the summer ahead. Making lists of things to do was a way to cope, but she needed to figure out a way to do more than that, there needed to be some resolution to her situation.

Steve was waiting on her doorstep. He reached down and picked up something as she got out of the car, flowers.

"Hi." He said as he handed her the flowers.

She looked at them, then at him, then back to the flowers. "Thank you." She said quietly.

He reached out his hand and forced her to look up at him. Her eyes were filled with tears. He hesitated only a moment, then gathered her in his arms. She rested comfortably there.

"I'm sorry," he said.

"I missed you," she said. And it was clear to her that she couldn't abandon Steve on the flimsy hope of a dream. She loved Chase, but needed Steve. Would her terms be acceptable to him? She drew away. "Have you eaten yet?"

"No. Let's go out."

"No, let's not. I can put together a pizza and salad in a few minutes. Come on in."

They made dinner together, talking about their week. But Katie was just waiting for him to begin asking questions. After they had eaten, they sat together on the porch, watching the last of the day disappear.

"What's going on?" He asked.

She looked at him in question.

"You can't avoid this forever, you know. I know you well enough. Look at the evidence. First, you took off early Sunday morning without a word to anyone. And you forget, you have been keeping me informed of your plans. Second, when I called you on Monday, you snapped at me. That was the first time you weren't honest with me. Even if I don't like what you say, you are always honest with me. That's one of the things I like about you. Third, you never tried to get in touch with me all week. Again, unlike you. I thought I could trust you. You can't change in mid-step and think I won't notice. I thought we had an understanding. What's the problem?"

Katie didn't say anything, but pressed closer to him. He put his arm around her.

"Katie," he spoke softly. "What is it?"

His hand gently turned her head until she was looking into his gold flecked eyes. What could she say? How could she tell him what had been going through her head? She didn't want to hurt him. Yet, if she were honest with him, it would be impossible not to. She either told him or she didn't trust him. His arm once comforting now felt like a vice. She got up and went into the house. He followed her into the living room.

At his hurt and bewildered look, she said, "I'm sorry Steve. I don't want to hurt you."

He was silent. Then, "What is it? What happened to us?"

Silence weighed heavily on the air. She closed her eyes. She tried to find the words to answer his questions. But she didn't have the answers. In frustration, more than anything else, she started to cry. She wiped the tears away angrily. Now was no time to cry.

Steve stood watching her, trying to figure out what to do. "Come here." He commanded.

She hesitated only a moment and he pulled her against him. She couldn't stop crying. She was so tired. There were so many tears waiting to be shed. After a while the tears exhausted themselves. He handed her his handkerchief and she blew her nose.

"I'm sorry, Steve. I've been very confused." She paused. "I had a nightmare Saturday night. It threw me off, way off. And you threw me off, too." She looked into his serious blue eyes.

"I did?"

Yes." She extracted herself from his arms and went to the window. It was dark now.

She turned back to him. "You took me by surprise when you said I love you." She looked at him, standing tall and lean with his wild blond hair and blue eyes. She was attracted to him, no doubt. "I don't know, Steve." She paused. "I guess I felt overwhelmed. You scare me. So I left. I went home."

"Now?" He asked.

"And now?" He came to her. "Do you know now?"

"No. I don't have any more answers now than I did last week." She reached up to kiss his cheek, seeking to soften the blow of her words. Looking into his gold flecked eyes she softly added, "I missed you, this week. I have fun with you and you make me feel valued. But…"

"Why don't you just say it?" He said quietly and moved across the room.

"What?"

"You don't love me. You never will. You've got a lot of unsolved issues and you're just hiding behind me and avoiding dealing with them."

She heard the anger in his voice.

"Yes, that's partially true, but still a stretch." She went to him and took him by the shoulders. "I'm sorry. I'm not as sure as you are. What can I say? Maybe it seems like I make everything more difficult than it need be. But you push pretty hard."

The anger left his face. "I'm sorry, Katie." He murmured as he pulled her close. "I'm just so anxious, so worried that I might lose you. I keep trying to tear down your walls when you're probably more comfortable with them coming down bit by bit." He pulled back to look at her. "Just relax. Don't think so much. Just let things go, let it happen. Don't fight it so much."

His words made sense.

"I'll try." She whispered.

"Try. That's all I ask." He paused and their eyes held. He

must have sensed the uncertainty there or tiredness; she didn't know which was more powerful. He leaned and lightly kissed her on the cheek and left.

#

Father's Day weekend found Katie on the way home to the farm. She hadn't exactly invited him along. When she told him she was going away for the weekend, he said he wanted to come with her, she didn't object and so he did.

"Come on Misty. Get in the car," Katie said. Misty jumped into the back seat and they were off. It was Friday evening. She hadn't seen him since Saturday. They weren't seeing as much of each other. Something had changed. He was slowly withdrawing. When they were together he kept his mask on. She never knew what was on his mind. Except when he kissed her good night. Then she felt like he was kissing someone else, it was so different. His kiss was very short, very light. He didn't ask anything in return from her.

Steve wanted so much more than she was ready or willing to give. She didn't know if she ever would or could. So, she decided to let him go. Yet here he was going to meet her parents.

Steve was tired tonight. There were shadows under his eyes and his face looked drawn. He had begun to work even longer hours than his already full schedule. His explanation was that with the continued cuts to the Legal Service Corporation the office was understaffed even though the case load was growing. She couldn't argue with a reason like that, everyone knew programs were being cut. So, she didn't say anything.

She felt, though, he was trying to fill her place with work. He thought he could hide it from her. But she knew him well enough. She didn't say anything though. She had already said enough.

It was such a game, she thought. Life was a total game. It was. It didn't matter how honest you were with the players, it was still a game. Honesty is just part of the game, too. It didn't matter if you won or lost. It was how you played it. And some of the rules were rather unclear. They were just playing a game with each other. He had already showed his hand. At some point the game would end. It couldn't go on this way much longer. Who the biggest loser would be, she didn't know.

She looked out her window as they drove out of her driveway. Rose hips were in bloom.

"What are you thinking about?" Steve asked.

"Stuff."

"Still thinking too much." He turned his full attention to the road. She watched him drive. She missed him, but she couldn't give him what he wanted.

They had the windows down. He rested one arm on the car door, casually steering with his thumb and forefinger. His other arm was at his side. The wind was rifling his hair. She wanted to reach out and be close to him again.

She didn't. Instead she focused her attention out the front window. Traffic was light.

"So, did you reach any conclusions?" He asked.

"About what?"

"Stuff? Life? That is what you were thinking about isn't it?"

"Oh. No." Here we go again, she thought. She could feel the tension begin to fill the air, could feel it in the pit of her stomach.

"Have you figured out what it is?" He asked, pushing her.

She didn't answer. She had no answer.

He looked at her. His eyes were hard. She thought for a couple of minutes, their eyes holding. She could feel his anger. She had to be gentle. "Steve, don't push me."

He looked back at the road, "Quit avoiding the issue."

"What issue? Us? I'm not avoiding the issue. You're here with me." She said emphatically. "Going with me to meet my parents. Now, why don't you tell me what's really on your mind. If you want to talk about something, then let's talk about it. Otherwise, quit trying to pick a fight with me. I don't need it. Not from you."

He didn't say anything. He kept his eyes to the road. He rolled up his window and turned the radio on.

Katie could feel her heart beating. She watched him drive, waiting to see if he'd look at her. When he didn't, she turned and watched the miles roll by out of her window. She fought to get her emotions back under control. Misty stuck her head over her shoulder, pushing her nose out the side window. Katie reached up and petted her. At least she had Misty. It seemed that Steve was almost gone, but that was part of her decision. Why did he want to meet her family this weekend? What was he thinking?

It was at the last faint light of day when they arrived at the farm. Except for when Katie gave Steve directions to the farm, they hadn't spoken the rest of the trip. But by the time they got home she was in control of herself again. Things were not going well, now. But they had the weekend to get through.

Martha and Alex Carlson came out of the house at the sound of the car doors slamming. Katie took Steve's hand as they walked towards them, trying to look as if everything were perfectly normal. "Mom, Dad, this is Steve."

Alex was his friendly self. He smiled and shook Steve's hand. "It's nice to meet you. We've heard so much about you."

Steve looked at her with faint amusement. "It's good to be here. Katie has told me so much about you and the farm. I feel like I've known you for a long time."

Katie wondered at the things that came out of his mouth. He sure was smooth.

"Why don't you come in. I've got a snack ready." Martha said, always so gracious.

They all trouped into the house and made small talk over ice cream and strawberries and coffee.

"Where's John tonight?" Katie asked.

"Oh, he went to town to the races with a bunch of his old high school friends." Martha said and went on to inform them of all the activities and whereabouts of John's friends for the last five years. One glance at Steve's face told Katie his thoughts were elsewhere. She started to feel the tension rise again. She tried to be cheerful and talkative, asking questions of Martha, but she failed miserably. Talk finally sort of died out and Martha began to clear the dishes. Katie rose to help her and she said, "No, you stay there. Dad will help me." Martha and Alex left them alone.

Katie looked over at Steve. He was looking at her thoughtfully, as if he was trying to figure something out. She smiled and shrugged. She couldn't begin to imagine what he was thinking. So far things the weekend had not been going that well. Question was, would it get better? Why did Steve come here anyway?

His face cleared up and he leaned across the table. "Let's go for a walk. I want to talk."

They got up.

"Mom," Katie called. "We're going for a walk."

They went out. The dogs were totally enjoying themselves. Misty ran up with Skippy and Huey like she was trying to say, "See. See my new friends." They stopped to pet them, but they kept running around fighting for their attention. They ignored them.

"Well," she said, trying to keep her voice light. "Where do you want to go? You have a choice. Either out the driveway to the road or behind the grove to the pasture."

"The grove sounds much more romantic." He took her hand.

They walked around the grove in silence. Romantic, she

wondered. What was on his mind now? She'd settle for a little honesty. But then, was she ready to be honest with him? Again? It had only left pain before. He felt her tension and squeezed her hand gently. They reached the big hill in the pasture. There was a full moon and the surrounding countryside was bathed in its light.

"Katie," he said softly, gently.

She turned to face him, her stomach tightening.

He took her hands and their eyes held. She didn't move a muscle. His eyes were intense, the gold flecks were sparkling. He didn't speak. Whatever it was he wanted to say wasn't coming to his lips easily.

Into his eyes crept a question. She felt herself responding and slowly they moved together until their lips met. It was a long kiss, filled with many meanings. First it was intense, like their earlier conversation. Then it was forgiving and finally caring. The feelings they had held in their shells, for whatever reason were unleashed. When the kiss ended, he held her close.

"I'm sorry I've been so hard on you," Steve began. But she cut him short.

"It's okay," she said. "I understand."

He looked at her in surprise. "You do?"

"Yes." She said quietly.

He thought about it for a while, and then he said in a low voice, as if afraid to voice his thought. "You were letting me go?"

She didn't say anything.

"Why?"

14

Fourteen

She took a deep breath. An honest conversation she had wanted, but was she ready? It had to happen sometime. This was as good a time as any. "Because I can't give you what you want from me. Because I don't know if I could ever love you the way you want me to love you. Because all I seem to do these days is hurt you and I don't like that. So I figured it was easier to let you go. At some point it seemed it was going to happen so I thought why delay the inevitable. Why pretend something that isn't and might never be. You've made it pretty clear how you feel, Steve. You've set out your expectations pretty clearly. And all I'm doing is frustrating you. Hurting you. I'm not ready to move as fast as you are. I need time. I've told you that and yet…" her voice trailed off.

"I keep pushing you." He filled in.

"Yea. It's your character. Your nature. That's one of the things I like about you. You set your sights on something and you push until you get it. It's probably worked for you most of the time. And we probably wouldn't be here right now if you hadn't pushed your way into my life last February." She smiled sadly. "But I can't be pushed where my heart is not ready to go."

He stopped her then by pulling her roughly to him. "I know I've pushed you. I'm sorry. It's just that. Oh hell. I'm not used to being held back. It's an adjustment for me." He moved his hand up until he was lightly holding her face, forcing her to meet his eyes. She waited for him to go on. "These last few weeks have been awful. I've missed you. I love you. I need you. I'm at a loss trying to figure out how to win you."

"Maybe you're trying too hard."

"Maybe. Maybe you're just afraid to love."

"Maybe."

"Well," he stopped. "Well," he said again. "I'll try not to push you so hard. And if whoever you fell in love with last fall comes back I won't stand in the way. But don't be afraid of love. "

He leaned forward and kissed her. A kiss filled with tenderness and longing.

Later she lay in bed and thought about his words. What did they mean for her? She tried to draw up Chase's picture. She couldn't.

#

On Saturday morning Alex showed Steve around the farm. Martha and Katie stayed in the house and lingered over coffee together. They didn't speak for a while. Katie was still dwelling on what Steve had said. She was relieved to have his friendship back, but things were by no means settled. Chase's face had eluded her for the first time in weeks. That bothered her. She frowned.

"How are things going after your walk last night? What time did you come in?" Martha asked.

"Not too late. Did you hear us?"

"I always do."

"We tried to be quiet." Katie paused a few more seconds before answering her mom's first question. "Things are better than they were. We've not been seeing that much of each other since I was down here last. And then we've been arguing a lot. Yesterday, driving down we didn't talk except to argue." She frowned again. "He's made it pretty clear how he feels and what he wants from me. And I'm not ready for him. I don't know if I ever will be. And that's hard for him. He's not use to waiting for what he wants. He's been pushing me and I've held firm. Last night, finally, we talked about it. I was honest with him. I told him I didn't know if I could ever feel the way he does."

"It must have gone okay. You guys are a lot more relaxed this morning."

"Well, you know I'm never good at pretending. He told me I'm afraid to love. I told him maybe he was right. I think that's the part he liked. It gave him wiggle room." Katie smiled briefly. A good attorney always liked a bit of wiggle room.

They were silent for a while, each lost in their own thoughts. Martha was assessing what she learned and evaluating her impressions of Steve. Katie, on the other hand, was trying to decide what difference their conversation made in their relationship. Did he really mean it when he said he loved and needed her but would let her go when Chase came back? Was that the ultimate love? The kind where you loved someone so much you put them before you, no matter how much it hurt? She found that hard to believe. If he really loved her, he would give her time and space and he would fight to win her love, not just let her go. She realized that she remained uncomfortable about their relationship. Nothing had been resolved out in the pasture last night. It wasn't as simple as he thought. You couldn't just love someone, and then let them go.

It wasn't right. No. No matter that she valued his friendship, enjoyed his company and his kisses. She should let him go. He loved her. She didn't love him, more to the point, she wasn't sure really how much he loved her. She should let him go. She shook her head. It was something she had been avoiding for a long time.

As she got up to refill their coffee cups, she caught Martha studying her. She knew her too well. Katie smiled and handed her a cup.

"You're still not certain about him?" Martha asked.

"No. I'm not." She paused. "I'm thinking it might be better if we quit seeing each other altogether. You know, quit dating."

Martha hesitated only a moment. "Hmm. What of Chase? Have you heard from him? Have you tried to reach him? How do you feel?"

"No. I haven't heard from him. I don't expect too. I'm not sure about trying to reach him? That's kind of scary now. I don't know. But I do feel the same way, but you know, I'm having a hard time remembering his face. You know the memory that you carry with you. It's eluding me."

"Well, it's been a long time."

"Yes. It has." Almost a year, she thought. That's a long time to carry around a piece of hope for something you aren't completely sure existed outside your own imagination.

"You know, you were awfully sick when you got home. Isn't, couldn't," she paused. "Maybe you just imagine you love Chase."

Katie looked at her hard. She had voiced the very core of the issue, her imagination. "Maybe," she said. She could feel her stomach begin to tighten up. She didn't want to think about it. Was it only her imagination? Or was it real? Could her imagination create such strong feelings? The doubts went round and round. "I don't know, Mom," she said. "I hope not. I just can't fathom. . ." She couldn't finish the thought, instead she finished her coffee.

"I'm sorry. I didn't mean to upset you. I just thought of it."

"Well, I've thought of it before, and I go in circles." She laughed without humor. "You know, Steve says I think too much. Well, I try not to think about this. I even try not to think about Chase." She took a deep breath and stood up. "I'm going for a bike ride." She took her cup and put it in the sink.

"I don't think you should go without Steve." Martha said.

Katie paused a moment before going out the door. "I suppose you're right." She shrugged and left to find Steve. He and Alex had just finished their tour and she met him as she was heading down to the farm yard.

"I'm going for a bike ride. Care to come along and get a tour of the neighborhood?" She asked Steve.

"Sure. Why not?"

Within minutes they were heading down the driveway. "We'll go around the section." Katie said. "It's about four miles and all gravel. Sound okay?"

"Yeah. I'm glad we have mountain bikes."

They rode in silence, listening to the sounds of the countryside. They could hear the dull rumble of tractors cultivating, smell the fresh cut hay, hear the morning doves' call and the frogs calling from the low spots. The sky was a perfect cornflower blue with little wisps of clouds floating along. It was a glorious summer morning in the country. The air was fresh and light, no hint of a storm.

Finally, as they approached the home stretch she screwed up her courage. "Steve." She said. "Can I ask you why you decided to come home here with me this weekend? You never did say."

"I wanted to meet your folks. See where you grew up. I figured it may give me some insight."

"Into me?"

"Yeah. Because I thought it might help me understand you. In case you didn't notice, I'm feeling kind of desperate"

"Umm. Ahh." She paused. "You know, I really appreciated last night. I thought we reached a tentative conclusion. We talked about you trying not to push and me trying to be open. But when you tell me you're feeling desperate, I feel panic. And then we argue. You want to argue now, I can tell. I still feel the same about things this morning. I'm not sure I'm comfortable to continue seeing you in a dating relationship. I've got a lot of projects this summer I need to do." She pushed on, rushing to finish before she lost her courage. "In fact, I'm going to New York in July to meet with the publishers of my new book. Did I tell you they liked it? Well, the last time I did a book we handled it all my phone and email. This time they'd like me to spend some time in the city. They're interested in signing a contract for future books. I'm really excited about it. I've always wanted to develop my writing career and do less teaching. This may be my big chance."

"I see. You've got this all figured out, don't you." It was a statement, not a question and she could feel his growing frustration and anger.

"No. I don't. But sometimes I feel like having a relationship with you is like trying to fit a square peg into a round hole. Look," she pressed on. "I like you a lot. I have fun with you. I like being with you. I appreciated last night. I enjoy you. But you always want more. You push. I pull. We fight. This isn't fun. It should be fun. Let's back off and just be friends. Get together from time to time."

"And then maybe?"

"You're pushing again. Maybe is perhaps better for you and someone else. Maybe you can just think about this for a while and let me know."

"Okay. I'll think about it. It won't do much good as near as I can tell." He gave his bike a hard pedal and pulled in front and away. When he reached the Carlson's driveway he kept going straight, leaving her in his dust.

When Katie reached the driveway, she stopped. There were no tears. Her heart was heavy. But underneath it all there was a certain sense of freedom. She knew Alex would be sad they were leaving so soon and she knew Martha would understand. It was for the best, no matter what the future held.

#

In mid-July, Katie stuffed her coat in the overhead compartment then squeezed by the large man in the aisle seat, the middle seat, was empty and sat by the window. She put her carry-on bag beneath her seat. She placed her book bag on the floor by her feet, leaning it against the wall. She was on her way back to Minnesota from New York. She leaned back in satisfaction. The ground crew put the luggage on the conveyor to the hold of the plane. Soon, she looked at her watch; they'd be in the air.

The week had flown by in a whirl wind of meetings with publishers. Her manuscript she had worked on all winter was held in high regard. They signed her to a two-year, two book contract and the financial terms were good too. Icing on the cake.

Yes, she had every reason to be pleased with herself. She had worked hard and it paid off. She met her goal. Yet, she felt restless. She looked down at her brief case. Chase Harrington's most recent book was in it.

She had been browsing in a small bookstore off of Madison Avenue on Friday when she saw his name staring up at her in bold print. She stopped, reached out, picked it up and turned it over. There on the back cover was his picture. His hair was longer, but still the soft dark waves curled around his ears. He wasn't smiling. She looked closer at his eyes. They were all she remembered and more — dark pools that made her forget all else. But something was wrong. What was it?

"May I help you?"

She almost jumped. It was a sales clerk. She mumbled something, bought the book and left. Outside she stopped to get her bearings. It was time for her last meeting with the publishers, which went by in a blur. She couldn't wait to open the bag from the bookstore.

Finally, late in the day when they said their goodbyes, she went back to her hotel. She didn't feel like being alone in her room so she went down to the hotel's dining room. After she had placed her order, she opened the bag and pulled out the book. Instead of looking at Chase's picture she opened the cover and read the inside flap. Then she paged over to the table of contents.

Her hand shook as she sipped her wine. It was an enticing book, unlike anything Chase had ever written before. It was a philosophical, historical exploration of the values he expressed in his earlier writings. This book gave depth and meaning to the other works — even though they were significant in their own right. This one gave the basis. Faith. Not just any faith, faith in God and how this faith played out in American culture. Where it mattered, where it didn't and where it should.

She ate without tasting, paging through the book. Then she turned to the back inside cover. There she read Chase's brief biography — New York born, raised, educated, attorney, lecturer, and address: Oregon. No mention of family. She closed the book. His haunting dark eyes stared up at her.

As she finished her dinner, she glanced at the book laying there. Then opening it to the back cover she read once again his biography. Thoughtfully, she turned to check the publishing date. Last month. She looked at Chase's picture on the book again. She was looking for something. Something was wrong. She shook her head. Maybe it was just her. Maybe her imagination was looking for something to be wrong. She signed her check and left. She decided to wait and read the book, cover to cover, when she got home, when she had more time.

15

Fifteen

Now Katie was on her way home and she hadn't been able to shake that restless feeling. She looked back from the window. The middle passenger had arrived. "Hi." She said, then looked back out the window. The ground crew was finished. She felt her neighbor settle in. She glanced sideways at him. She guessed him to be in his late twenties. He was dressed in a dark blue business suit, a blue buttoned-down shirt with a maroon tie. He had short cropped blond hair, he was clean shaven. The only thing that didn't fit his New York image was his wire rimmed glasses. Behind those glasses was a pair of dull brown eyes.

The plane began to taxi. She put some gum in her mouth and began to chew. Her ears always got plugged. She saw her neighbor glance at the gum so she offered him a piece.

"Thanks." He said. "My ears always get plugged up."

She smiled. "So do mine."

"Leaving New York?" He asked.

She nodded.

He eyed her book bag. "Here on business?"

"Sort of."

"What do you do?"

"I teach at a small college in Minnesota."

"What do you teach?"

"U.S. History, intellectual history and contemporary affairs."

"Sounds interesting."

"It is." Who is he kidding? Not that many people were into my line of work, she thought as she looked out the window. They were passing through the dark clouds into sunlight. She glanced at her watch, 8 p.m. Would they follow the sunset home? She looked at her book bag again. She didn't want to start reading the book yet. But she was propelled by something stronger than reason. She took it out.

"Is that new?" Her neighbor asked.

"Yes." She looked at him in surprise.

"Do you mind?" He already had the book in his hand and was looking it over. Then he opened it, as she had, read the front and back inside covers and then the table of contents. He handed it back. "Looks good."

The stewardess came and gave them their pop and peanuts. Katie pulled her tray down, placing her glass on it. She could tell her New York neighbor wanted to talk more. So she opened the book and casually paged through the first few pages to the table of contents. She noticed it was dedicated to Kaycee. She pretended to read the table of contents. Her fingers itched to turn to the beginning of the book. She closed it and laid it face down on the table. She took a drink of her diet pop. Chase's face stared up at her.

"Have you read any of his stuff?" Her neighbor pointed to Chase.

"Yes."

"Pretty good." He commented. "What do you think?" He regarded her with his brown eyes. She looked down at the book.

"I think he's an excellent writer. I use one of his earlier books in my contemporary affairs class. He makes you think." Is that why I love him? He makes me think? She wished she knew.

He said something.

"What?" She asked. She wanted to read, not discuss Chase Harrington or any of his books.

"I met him this spring. He was in New York for meetings."

"Did you?" She hoped her voice was normal. She was suddenly more than interested in discussing Chase. She casually looked out her window again. They were riding the clouds with the sunset. Clouds formed the horizon. And they were deep purple, lavender, pink, some white and others were touched with gold. It was beautiful.

He was talking. She brought her attention back and pretending her ears were plugged said, "Pardon?"

"I said," he was talking too loudly. "I met him at a dinner

party some friends of mine gave. He's a lawyer you know. Has a degree anyway. I don't know how much he practices."

She wondered if the New Yorker was a lawyer.

"Very interesting guy." He paused remembering. "He wore blue jeans. We all had business suits on. Yet, he wasn't out of place. Strange. The host of the party, I guess, was a friend of his. It was to be some sort of celebration. Probably for this book. But something wasn't quite right. He was very quiet, didn't engage much in the conversation around him. If I knew him better I might say he didn't look very happy."

"That would be odd, wouldn't it? I mean, if he just finished his book, you'd think he'd have been pretty happy." She fingered the book. "I know if I worked that hard on something, I'd be happy and relieved when it was finished and on its way to be published. Did you hear what was the matter with him?" She pictured Chase. He probably wasn't unhappy. New York dinner parties weren't exactly his style. He would have been quiet but his eyes would have been alive and dancing. That was it! She looked at Chase's picture. His eyes were lifeless. Something drained out of her. Vaguely she heard her neighbor talking.

"Somebody said it was a woman."

She looked at him in surprise. "A woman?"

"I didn't know for sure. I didn't talk to him at all. But that's what other people were saying."

Katie didn't want to hear anymore, he either didn't notice, or didn't care. He just kept on talking. "I find it hard to believe myself. I'd heard of Chase Harrington. He has something of a reputation. It's incredible." He laughed. "Even at this party, there were beautiful women. He ignored them. So I doubt that rumor. He's arrogant and aloof. He writes well, but I don't think he can handle people."

Katie looked out the window again, her stomach in knots.

"He has a cabin in Oregon, you know," he continued. "I did hear he spends a lot of time there."

"We all have our escapes." Katie said.

He continued, "He didn't this year, which was unusual. He had to travel to write his book, they were saying. If I was going to write a book, I'd stay out of sight, I'd stay at a cabin in the mountains. No, something doesn't quite add up. I wonder how good this new book really is?"

She focused on the beautiful sunset in the clouds. He didn't need an audience, if he wanted to continue to talk, he could. She had heard enough.

Her heart went out to Chase. The guy sitting next to her was in the wrong section. He belonged in First Class. He was a first-class jerk. Imagine telling everyone he encountered every rumor he ever heard about someone. He probably wasn't a lawyer, at least not a successful one. He probably was a salesman for a string company.

She laughed to herself. Chase wasn't cold. He was warm and tender. He was honest and good. She could see him being thought of as aloof in a strange crowd. But arrogant? No, not intentionally. Chase was an introvert and it made him seem aloof. He had been aloof from her at times, distant and brooding. She looked at his picture. Those eyes, they were so empty. What had happened to him?

The excitement and the stress of the trip overwhelmed her. She leaned her head against the seat and stared, without seeing anymore the cloudy sunset. Chase was very much a part of her. Will I always have Chase in the corner of my heart? She thought. Will I be satisfied with only the memory of him? A memory that hurt every time she let it out. Could a dream become real? She needed to decide. It was time. She couldn't run anymore. She closed her eyes.

Katie woke up with a start. She thought she was flying through the air. But the plane was simply making its descent into the Minneapolis/St. Paul airport. They were coming in from the southeast. She could see the Mall of America. She took a deep breath, trying to clear her ears. It didn't work. She felt fatigued, disoriented.

"Are you alright?" The man from New York asked.

Her head cleared right away. "I'm fine. Thank you." She said. She didn't encourage conversation. The plane touched down.

Steve would be there to meet her. She had made her decision. She hoped he would understand. Though they only saw each other occasionally, she knew he still had hopes and plans. He wanted her.

She picked up Chase's book to put it away. But first she flipped through the first few pages to see if there was anything else she missed. She noticed the dedication, "To

Kaycee," again and wondered briefly who Kaycee was. Then they were ready to deplane.

She didn't even say good-bye to the New York string salesman in the blue suit. She looked for Steve as she made her way to baggage claim area. All those faces, looking for another. It was confusing. Somebody shouted her name. She stopped. Leave it to Steve to make a scene, she thought. She turned and there he was, coming with open arms. He hugged her, bags and all.

"How was New York? Did you meet with success?"

Despite her unsettling trip home, she couldn't hide her satisfaction. She grinned. He hugged her again. Then he took her carry-on bag. "Do you have checked luggage?"

She nodded, still smiling. It was good to be home.

"Well, let's go then." He started off toward the far end of baggage claim. He looked over at her and grinned. His blond hair was tousled as usual. "It's good to see you."

"It's good to see you, too." She said quietly.

Steve was whistling a light tune under his breath. "How was your flight?" He asked.

"Something else. I'm glad to be off it. I'll tell you about it later. You'll be really interested." She could safely tell him about what the New Yorker had said and show him Chase's new book. There was going to be more she would have to tell him. She didn't like it, any of it. She had told him at the farm how she felt. And he had given her space, lots of it. But when they were together, he still pushed. He was confident he could win her heart. He still didn't understand. Her heart was not hers to give. She shook her head, she had tried.

Katie caught Steve trying to get her attention. The devils were in his eyes. She laughed and took his hand. She wouldn't say anything tonight. She was too tired. But she would have to soon, before she went to Oregon. Her stomach tightened up in excitement. She was scared.

She finally made the decision. She decided to find out if her love for Chase was real or a figment of her imagination. She needed to discover if Chase felt anything for her. She needed to know these things in order to bring peace to her mind. To really get on with her life, she needed to know. And, if need be, to rid herself of Chase's haunting image.

They got Katie's luggage and went to Steve's car. "Did you get dinner on the plane?" Steve asked as they pulled out of the airport parking ramp onto Highway 5.

"No. They don't really serve meals on planes anymore do they? What time is it now? I'm hungry."

"10:30. didn't you eat before you took off?"

"No. But I'm hungry now."

He looked at her carefully. "I thought you looked thinner. I can see it in your face. Didn't they feed you?"

"It was really busy. Besides I think I could stand to lose some weight."

"I think you could stand to gain some. It seems you've been losing weight since I've known you. But do what you want. I learned long ago not to argue with a woman about her weight."

"Thank you. And you shouldn't argue with a woman about her career goals." She couldn't help but add. He hadn't been too happy with her going off to New York. But he had no choice. She was determined to go, and go alone. Despite how she maybe appeared to him, she was strong. And she would need every ounce of her strength for the next trip. The trip to Oregon, and Chase.

They pulled into the Happy Chef Restaurant in Shakopee about a half an hour later. Inside they ordered coffee and breakfast. After the waitress brought water and coffee Steve asked, "Well, when are you going to tell me about your trip? Tomorrow?"

"I'm sorry." She said. "Why didn't you say something in the car?"

"You seemed lost in thought." He was smiling.

"I was." She paused and studied his face a moment. Yet, there was an anxiousness waiting just beyond his smile. She took a sip of coffee. "Where do you want me to start?"

He frowned in exasperation and leaned forward. "Did they like your book?"

"Yes." She took another drink of coffee. She knew that short answers would drive him up the wall.

"How did it go?"

She smiled at him affectionately, and then told him everything. She told him about the meetings with the publishers, the book contracts and everything she saw and did. He kept after her for details and by the time their food arrived he knew everything she had done as if he had been there himself. Except she held back about Chase's new book, the conversation on the flight back and her decision. She would tell him most of that on the rest of the way home.

They continued talking about New York. Steve had stories of his own to share. The anxious look was gone. Although she appeared relaxed, there was a tension as well, as she kept a tight rein on her emotions. She had a dream to dispel, or make real, and until she did she had to continue to keep her distance from him. She watched his face carefully as they ate and talked. She should feel lucky to have him want her, instead she felt sad. Fortunately, it was time to leave and he didn't notice her shift in moods.

When they were back traveling on 169 south Katie said, desperately hoping she sounded normal even though her heart was pounding, "Chase Harrington has a new book out." It still struck her as ironic that Steve and Chase had been best friends in law school.

"Does he? Did you find it in New York?"

"Yes."

"Figures. What's it about."

"From what I can tell, it's the basis of all his writings. It is a philosophical, historical exploration of American culture and its relationship to faith in God."

"That's different, isn't it, from his other books?"

"Well, in a way yes, and in a way no. His other books dealt with specific issues. He mainly focused on natural resources in a historical context; how they were discovered, developed, technological changes, their continued availability and future outlook. He always came from the same perspective or formula, if you will. No, Contemporary Affairs goes much deeper than that. It is the philosophical, spiritual perspective from which he wrote his other books."

"You sound like you've read the book already."

"No, just the inside cover and table of contents. But you forget how well I know all his other books."

"Are you going to use it in your class?"

"Maybe. I'll have to read it first though, before I decide. See how it fits in. I'm thinking about restructuring my courses anyway, see if I can afford to reduce my class load now that I have the book contracts in hand."

They were silent. Steve absorbed the news that Katie was making some career changes as a result of her trip. Katie was thinking about the guy on the plane and what he had said about Chase. She wondered if Steve could shed any light on it. "I sat next to a guy on the plane who saw Chase. Harrington." She almost just said Chase. "At a dinner party last spring."

"Really? How did you find that out?"

"I had the book out and was looking at it. This guy, you wouldn't believe him, grabbed the book out of my hand, read the flaps and the proceeded to tell me all about this dinner party where he saw Chase Harrington. I guess he caused quite a stir."

"Who? Chase?"

"Yes."

"Why? I find that hard to believe."

"Well for one thing, he wore blue jeans and ignored all the beautiful women who were eying him."

Steve laughed. "That sounds like Chase, never one to follow convention. And he always pulls it off with style." He paused remembering. "And for some reason women always find him fascinating. It's his dark looks and his eyes. Women can't resist him, but he's always stayed unattached."

Katie tried not to be too interested. "Why is that, do you know?"

"I remember him telling me once. It's not something he talked much about, you know." He paused. "He's an introvert and sensitive. He takes everything to heart." He looked over. "Like you."

"Oh."

"Anyway," he continued. "It makes him seem aloof, even arrogant at times." He paused peering into the night. "Back to the woman thing. It's an old story. The high school sweetheart. We all had one, only Chase never forgot, or forgave, I don't remember which."

"What happened? What was she like?" She hoped her question sounded ordinary.

"It's the same thing that happens to everyone at the age. He was most likely to succeed, you know, the class all-star. She was the class beauty — plus she was ambitious. Chase is laid back, he had a different set of values, even then. It wasn't going to work. But he was too young to see it, at the time." He shrugged. "It was a hard lesson. In college he poured himself into his studies. Then law school. He's been very driven, very successful. But like your New York friend said, I don't know if he's happy. He's achieved his success and yet he has a hard time trusting anyone. At least he was when I knew him, that's probably not changed by all indications. So he writes and teaches seminars at prestigious places, never really settling down." Steve shook his head. He looked at her. "Even at school, he kept to himself. He was my one of my best friends, yes, but that was because I forced myself on him."

Katie smiled to herself. She could see the always confident outgoing Steve building up Chase. But her impression of Chase differed. She didn't see a lonely man, but one who was at peace with himself and the world. He maybe was busy but he had a lot to say.

Steve continued, "and even then there was always that final barrier. No, I don't fully understand him." He was quiet for some time.

"Are you sleeping? Sorry, I kind of rambled, but it opened up a store of memories for me. Come here." He commanded. He reached across the seat for her and she slid next to him resting her head on his shoulder thinking about all he had said. She had been given a snap shot of the man who captured her fascination. Would he ever be real to her? Would he, when she saw him, let down his barrier? Would he let her in? Or would he draw back? Would he love her? She loved him. She knew it. She knew it. Would he love her? She sighed.

"Not much farther and we'll be home." Steve said.

"Good. I'm tired."

16

Chapter Sixteen

A little rain
always quiets
a raging storm.
Then comes a rainbow-
the sign of peace.
Then comes the sun-
the sign of love.

The first week of August Katie Carlson was heading west, to Oregon. This time her brother John brought her to the airport. Steve had been difficult. But he had no choice.

"Somehow I knew I could never keep you." He said. His blue eyes were sad and the gold flecks were gone. Her heart was in her throat. He saw. "Come here." He commanded one last time. She went to him and they held each other tightly. "You take care of yourself out there. Call me when you get back, if you want." He pulled away. Their eyes held a moment longer. "I might not be here when you get back." He said as he was leaving. Then he was gone.

She didn't cry as she watched him drive away. She had set her course. She knew what she needed to do. It scared her. She stared out the window a long time after he left. Then she finished packing.

There had been a couple of more visits to the farm. Martha and Alex were more than supportive. There was a lot they didn't understand, but they knew this was something she had to do. She had waited long enough. She had tried long enough to forget. But Chase was always there in the shadows. She couldn't move ahead with her life until she came to grips once and for all with the power he held over her. Martha was even a bit excited. She found it romantic, if a bit unusual. Katie told her she had been reading too many romance novels. But secretly, Katie believed it to be romantic too. Had been from the start, which again, in her mind, was part of the problem.

John was encouraging as they approached the airport for her flight to Portland, then Medford, Oregon. He gave her a hard hug when he dropped her off.

"Take care, Katie." He said. "I hope it works out the way you hope. I love you."

"Thanks, John, for everything. I'll be fine. I love you too. Bye."

"Bye."

With that she left. She was really on her way, at last. She

could hardly believe it. She took a deep breath, trying to calm down. The flight wasn't full and she had a window seat, but no seat mates to bother her. She was relieved. They were going to follow the sun again into the night. She pulled out a magazine. She would save her books for when she got to Chase's. She felt the excitement build again. Relax, she commanded herself. She looked out the window at the passing earth below. They were over South Dakota. From then on, she lost track.

She woke up with a start when she felt her stomach sinking into space. They were in Oregon. She had to change planes, rent a car and find a hotel before her journey this day would be over. Tomorrow another journey would begin.

Much later she settled into the same hotel as she had stayed at before her flight out of Oregon a year ago. The emotions of that moment were just as fresh. It was scary. She pulled out her map and traced her route for the following day. The next step of her journey was the first step toward the rest of her life. Maybe she was being too serious. She set the map aside and took a hot bath. Even so, she had a hard time falling asleep later. What was she going to say if he was there? What would she do if he wasn't there? And what would she do if he didn't want her to stay? How would things turn out? She tossed and turned. I'm here now, she told herself, I have to follow through. One way or another, she would have some answers. Finally, she slept.

#

Later the next day Katie stopped at the edge of a large

meadow. She wiped her face on her t-shirt, and then looked out across the open space. There was no sign of a cabin. She took off her pack to rest for a few minutes.

It was so quiet, so peaceful here. The mountain stood in sharp focus against the deep blue sky. She was tired. She had been climbing all day. She wiped her face again. She was a mess. Her face was all red and her hair was damp with sweat. She had carefully picked out her t-shirt and pants that morning, but hadn't given any consideration to the workout she would have getting to Chase's cabin. She remembered his comment about it being daunting to find him at the cabin. Daunting, huh, she thought, an understatement.

Well, it was too late now anyway. Her stomach tightened even more. It couldn't be too much farther. Her plan was good, but had taken longer to put into place than she had anticipated. She had searched out the forest service ranger station in the Mt. McLoughlin area where they had camped and hiked last year. She thought this was the same area that had coordinated the search and rescue efforts. She figured they'd know how to find the logging road to Chase's cabin. What she hadn't figured on was how many low maintenance logging roads there were in the area and how little record the forest service had of whom owned what private lands within the region. Finally, they tracked down someone who remembered the events of the previous fall, who knew Chase, who knew which forest service road to take to get to Chase's logging road.

Following what she thought were good directions, but

were in fact not, she found the fire number that the forest service said matched up to Chase's cabin and land. She parked her rental car; loaded up a few essentials and began to hike up the logging road. This was the second meadow she had to traverse. Luckily, you could see the outlines of the road through the prairie grass and she found the road on the other side. This second meadow was difficult. She wasn't sure if Chase's cabin or the road was on the other side.

The sun was getting ready to go behind the mountain. She put her pack back on and started across the meadow. This had to be the one. She didn't know what she was going to do if it became dark. After a while she saw the ridge rise sharply from the meadow, to the mountain.

By the time she reached the other side of the meadow the sun had disappeared and the shadows were long. She still didn't see a cabin. Nor did she see any evidence of a logging road or even a foot path. She took off her pack and sat down on a nearby rock to think through her situation. She did not want to admit she was lost, but she was, or nearly so. She pushed back the frustration that screamed at her for being so foolish. She had psyched herself up so much and now…where was she? She looked around. There were trees, rocks, grass, ridges, and bushes, no cabin.

She would have to set up camp here then start out again in the morning or, the thought trailed off. She didn't have a choice. It was almost completely dark. She needed to find a sheltered place to spend the night. She had a sleeping bag, but no tent. Another miscalculation, but fortunately it was

August, not October or even September. She should be fine in a sleeping bag. She left her pack and began looking for a flat grassy, sheltered place, but away from the openness of the meadow. It took a few minutes to find such a spot. When she found it, she took careful notice of the surroundings, then went back for her pack.

Just when she reached her pack she heard a dog bark. Something came crashing through the trees. She froze. As it came bounding through the trees she got a hold of herself and turned to run.

"Jake!" A voice yelled some distance away. Chase. Katie stopped dead in her tracks. Jake caught up to her, sniffing her. She petted his head, willing herself to be calm. A branch cracked and he ran off. Then he came back through the trees followed by Chase.

He stood there, silent for several seconds. And time actually seemed to stand still. He looked startled. Katie's heart was pounding so hard she was afraid he would hear it. She waited for him to say something, anything. The startled look was gone. "Well," he paused. She could see his eyes, guarded. "At least this time you're in one piece."

It was an effort, but she kept her voice steady and normal when she answered him. "Yes. But I think I'm lost."

"Oh?" He looked at her questioningly. "Where were you going?"

She felt her cheeks grow warm and was thankful for the darkness. This was why she had tossed and turned all night. It was now or never, she thought. "To find you," she answered simply.

"I see," he said quietly. "Well, here I am."

He stared at her a few more seconds. She wasn't sure if he was going to leave her there or not.

"Well, come on then. I said I'd rescue you anytime, so let's go." He said softly, and then before she could see his expression, he turned. She watched his hands as he reached out for her pack. They were large hands with long even fingers. She remembered how they had gently held her. He grasped the pack firmly and put it on his back. He adjusted it to fit. "What do you have in here?" He asked "Books?"

"Yes." She answered, feeling even more stupid.

"Really?" He looked closely at her. "Why?"

"I always bring a book or books with me, among other things."

"Oh." He seemed to consider something. "Well, let's get going, its getting too dark." He strode off up the ridge.

Katie had been wrong. The cabin wasn't in this meadow. She remembered looking out the kitchen window to the valley and out the living room windows to the mountain. She was confused, tired and could hardly see where she was going. She heard rather than saw Chase ahead of her. He wasn't following a trail.

As she tried to keep up with him, she wondered what he was thinking. It was an awkward start, but then she knew it would be. There was no easy way to walk into someone's life. Now that she was here she didn't know if she had enough nerve to follow through. At the moment, she just wanted to turn and run all the way back down the mountain. But no. She was here, she would stay. She ran once before. She would stay until he asked her to leave or until the end of next week, which ever came first. Then, she vowed, she would leave and never come back looking for Chase Harrington. She prayed that was a vow she wouldn't have to keep.

She stumbled in the darkness. A large root she hadn't seen caught her by surprise. She felt something give in her right ankle. She landed on her chest with her arms flung out in front of her. She lay still a moment catching her breath and swallowed her pride. Where was the strong independent woman? Flat on her face.

She heard Chase's footsteps then felt his hands as he helped her up. "Are you alright?" He asked. They were standing close, dirty and sweaty. But all she was aware of was where he had touched her and that he was only a half-step away. In the dim light, their eyes held for a long moment.

"I tripped. I'm fine." She said. "How much farther?"

His eyes remained on her for several seconds longer. She tore her eyes from his and peered around him into the night. She could feel her ankle begin to throb. She didn't want him to see the pain in her face.

"We're almost there. Over the top of this hill. Are you sure you're alright?" His voice held the concern she was so familiar with. But she didn't want his concern. She wanted him.

"Yes. I've fallen on my face before." She answered sharply.

He didn't laugh. "I know you have."

Her eyes flew to his face searching for an indication of his feelings. But his expression remained guarded.

He turned and continued climbing the ridge. She could feel her ankle swelling and throbbing, but she followed him. Some hill, she thought, ridge or small mountain would be more appropriate. At least as far as she could tell there still was no trail.

She simply couldn't hike, she limped behind him. Every step hurt. Finally, they reached the top of the ridge. It was another meadow, smaller than the one below. She looked for the cabin. But she couldn't see anything in the dark. Her ankle throbbed.

"Chase, can we stop a minute?" She couldn't mask her pain. She hobbled over to a large rock. She sat down, out of breath. She pulled up the bottom of her t-shirt and wiped off her face. Jake was nudging her. But she was watching Chase.

He stood there. He started to take off the pack, hesitated for a second. Before dropping it on the ground. He came over in one stride. Kneeling, he looked at her ankle. She could see the annoyance in his eyes when he looked up.

"Are you always this much trouble?" He muttered.

"Don't you know you're supposed to wear boots when you go backpacking?" He dropped her shoe and pulled off her sock. But his touch was gentle as he examined her ankle.

"This doesn't look good. How does it feel?"

"Like I sprained an ankle."

"This is the same one you sprained last year, isn't it?"

Of course, it was, she realized. He gave her sock back,

walked over, grabbed the pack and came back. He eyed her critically for a couple of seconds, thinking.

He smiled. "Now I'll have to carry you."

"No." She protested. "I can walk."

"I know you can. But it will be faster if I carry you. It's not far. We need to get that ankle up and iced. The less you walk on it now the sooner you'll walk on it again. Besides," he took her hand and pulled her to her feet. "I've carried you before." His tone was gentle but firm. She winced as her right foot touched the ground.

"Come on." He said again.

He stepped to her and lifted her easily, one arm supporting her back with the other under her knees. She hesitated a moment, then slipped her arms around his neck for balance. She was too close to him for comfort. Her heart was pounding and her senses racing. Despite the pain in her ankle, she was only aware of him.

"Relax. Will you." He said. "I'm not going to drop you." He looked down at her, his eyes the soft pools of her memories. Then he looked away. She relaxed and laid her head against his shoulder as she studied his face. Dark stubble covered a strong jaw line. A determined jaw line. She couldn't see his eyes, which was fine, she had seen enough already.

"Do you need to put me down?" She asked.

He looked down briefly. "No, we're almost there."

"Where?" She peered ahead into the night. "I don't see anything."

"You're not supposed to. There aren't any lights on."

"Where were you coming from when you found me? This time?"

He looked down again, this time he looked amused. "There's another meadow higher up. I go there sometimes for a day or two. There's no cabin, but I built a lean to shelter long ago. On my way back, Jake dashed off and down the ridge. To you." He looked down. "I followed."

"Oh." She said quietly, to herself.

"We're almost there." He said. In a minute she saw the shadow of the cabin. In two strides they were there. He let her feet slide to the ground as he braced her tight against him with his left arm. She could feel his heart beat evenly, smoothly beneath her own racing one.

"Ahh, Katie. I've missed you." He breathed with his other hand lost in her thick tangled hair. She became lost in his eyes. "I haven't had anyone to take care of since you left." He smiled slightly. Who takes care of you? She wanted ask.

"Here. Sit down for a couple of minutes. I'll be right back." He gently disengaged her arms from his neck.

The door slammed shut behind Chase. Jake sat down beside Katie and dropped his head on her lap. She draped her arms around him, wondering whatever in the world possessed her to come back. "Jake." She whispered into his ear, laying her cheek alongside his head. "What am I doing here?" She pulled back, her gray eyes troubled. She flopped his ears playfully, "huh?"

The door opened behind her and, as Katie looked into

Chase's face, she knew why. She could see him clearer in the light. He had almost a sheepish look about him. He stepped around her and she thought he was almost laughing. She could see it in his eyes.

"Ready?" He asked. She began to see what a comedy the situation was. Here she flies in from Minnesota, seeking her love without any thought for anything else. She hikes into the mountains, unprepared for the unexpected, gets lost, he finds her, she sprains an ankle and he has to carry her. All that was missing was the music.

He bent and swiftly gathered her up. She almost laughed. He climbed the steps and paused at the threshold looking down. He saw the laughter and his face broke into a smile.

"It is pretty funny isn't it?" He asked, reading her thoughts.

She smiled back. "Yeah. And I feel pretty stupid."

He laughed then, the laughter coming from deep inside him. She couldn't remember hearing him laugh before. She didn't laugh, but watched him closely. He stopped as suddenly as he started and looked down into her eyes. She felt herself get lost in the depths of emotions that were dancing there.

"Welcome again." He said softly. Then he leaned down and lightly touched his lips to hers. Before she could respond they were inside and he had kicked the door shut. He carried her to the couch. "Put your foot up on one of these pillows. I'll get some ice."

She leaned against the couch. Sighing she looked around. Nothing had changed. The desk was still cluttered, the pictures in the same place, the bookshelves full. Everything was neat and tidy and in place. A wave of tired anxiety washed over her. Why did she have to sprain her ankle? Why didn't she wear her hiking boots? Why? Why? Why? She caught her spiraling thoughts and brought them to a halt. This was her plan, she was here. She needed to stay calm. Otherwise, she would defeat her purpose without even trying.

She took off her shoes and placed her injured foot on the pillow Chase had thrown at her. She slid down until she was comfortable. Her ankle looked twice its normal size. She gingerly tried to extend and flex it. The tiny movement was impossible to complete. Searing pain raced from her ankle through the rest of her weary body. She winced and again fought back the frustration.

She could hear him clanging about and when he returned he had a bag of ice cubes in one hand and a kitchen towel in the other.

Chase gently placed the bag of ice on the swelling. Katie stiffened at the numbing coldness and bit at her lip. Chase took the towel and tied the ice in place. He left again and returned with two more pillows which he put under her foot. "You've got to keep it elevated in order to reduce the swelling." He told her.

He then brought her more pillows and a couple of blankets. He held them, considering her for a moment, his face uncertain. "I don't know what your story is and I don't want to hear it tonight. I have things I have to do." He handed her the extra pillows and began to open the blankets. "You might as well make yourself comfortable. You're not going to move for a while."

He began to tuck them in around her. She put her hand on his arm. "Can you wait a minute? I'd like to clean up. I'm a mess. And can you put my pack closer? And can I have a couple of aspirin and a glass of water?"

"Sure. Do you want anything to eat too?" He bent to pick her up. She pushed him back.

"I can walk if you will just help me get up and started."

She reached out for his hands and he pulled her easily up. In the end, he supported her to the bathroom and brought her pack. She washed up and changed into loose shorts and a clean t-shirt. Her ankle throbbed the whole time, but she felt somewhat better.

Chase wasn't around so she didn't wait and hopped and hobbled back to her spot on the couch. He heard her and came quickly from the kitchen in time to gently help her onto the couch.

"Thanks." She said gratefully. "I feel better."

"Good." He began tucking her in, repositioning the ice bag on her elevated right ankle.

"Chase. Can I have some aspirin and a glass of water?"

"I'm sorry." He left.

She sorted through her pack and found a book.

"You really do have a book in there?" Chase was back.

"Yes, thanks." She took the glass of water and the aspirin.

"Anything else?" He asked.

"No. I'll be all right tomorrow."

"We'll see." He said doubtfully. Then he smiled, his face lighting up briefly, a dimple tugging at the corner of his mouth. "Good night."

Katie met his gaze but could only manage a weary sad good night. She opened her book, but didn't see the words. She heard him turn to leave. She looked up as she said softly, "Chase." He stopped. "I'm sorry."

Their eyes held forever, then he shrugged. "Welcome back." He said and calling Jake disappeared into the kitchen.

Katie put her book down. The journey was well underway. The first day had used up nearly all of her reserves. She fell sound asleep, her injured foot sticking out of the blankets, water from the melting ice trickled out. She didn't feel it. Nor did she feel Chase remove the soggy bag from her ankle.

Katie didn't know Chase was glad to see her. He had missed her that was true. He felt something stir inside he thought he had safely buried. She didn't know that he ached to hold her, to feel her once again in his arms.

She was lost in the mountains because she was trying to find him. She was here. That's all that counted for now. He would figure out the rest out as he went along.

17

Seventeen

Katie's ankle was throbbing. She could feel the swelling. She opened her eyes. It was dark. She was covered by a heavy quilt, except for her right ankle, elevated and throbbing. She had no idea what time it was. All she knew was the pain was worse. She tried sleep. She couldn't. The pain along with the events of the day conspired to sweep the relief of sleep away.

Katie lay still, but felt restless. She fought the pain and restlessness for a long time. Finally, she couldn't take it. She threw back the quilt and swung around so she was sitting up. She felt the blood rush, pounding into her ankle. Searching the darkness of the cabin she soon began to make out the shadows. Where did he keep his aspirin? She wondered, in the kitchen above the sink or in the medicine cabinet in the bathroom? He had brought water and aspirin from the kitchen last night. She decided to try there.

Gingerly she stood. Pain shot through her. Now all she

had to do was get to the wall by the kitchen door and from there she could work her way to the kitchen sink. She figured out her route and within seconds was hopping across the room. She faltered once but regained her balance. Finally, she reached the wall. She leaned against it trying to catch her breath.

Then out of the darkness Chase inquired, "What do you think you're doing?"

Katie almost swore. She woke him up.

"Sorry." She said. "I didn't mean to wake you up."

"Just how, if I may ask, did you expect me not to?"

She wished she could just disappear. "I need some more aspirin. I can't sleep. I can't walk. So, I . . ." She trailed off as she slid down to the floor.

She heard him get up. A light came on and he came around the corner. He was only wearing jeans. His bare chest was tan and covered with curling black hair. She stared. She willed her eyes to his face. He was tousled and sleepy. She almost smiled, but caught herself. He didn't look angry, but she didn't want to push her luck. Then she noticed his mouth was relaxed and small smile playing at his lips. He ran his hand through his dark hair.

"What am I going to do with you?" He asked as he reached out a hand. He pulled her up. He held her eyes with his.

"Does your ankle really hurt that much?"

"Yes." She tried to stand on one leg, leaning against him for support.

He turned and helped her back to the couch. He sat down,

pulling her with him. She could feel her heart begin to pound and a whole new feeling began to warm her from the inside out. His eyes were soft pools; she lost herself in them as his lips met hers.

It was the kiss that sealed her fate. She knew instantly there would be no other for her but him. Even as she lost herself, she knew there were many things they had to sort out between them. This knowledge gave her strength to ease away. He wiped a strand of hair from her face.

"Feel better?" He asked softly.

She felt relief. She was right. She had been right to come back. "Yes." She said and reached out to trace the strong jaw as she had been so longing to do. He shifted her closer. She couldn't hide the wince. "And no." She added with a soft smile. "I really do need more aspirin. I wasn't making it up."

But he kissed her again anyway and then eased out from under her. He gently helped her settle back on the couch, placing her swollen ankle on the pillows. He saw the pain in her eyes,. "I'll be back in a minute."

Katie's world was soft and warm as she waited for Chase. When he returned she noted the tenderness which emanated from him. It was though she was looking through a filtered lens, which made everything smooth and soft, taking out the harsh lines. He was a dream. She yearned to be held by him forever. Instead she took the aspirin he held out to her.

"You have the greatest entrances," he whispered, as he tucked the blankets around her "Welcome home."

He kissed her again, tenderly and reluctantly left her.

Katie woke slowly. She could smell the fire taking the edge of the chill from the air. Chase was moving around the cabin. She heard him let Jake out. But she didn't open her eyes. She was still floating in that cloud of half sleep; and it was a warm and cozy world. She was vaguely aware of the pain in her ankle but let the fog of sleep thicken and it was gone again.

She was in a soft dream world where Chase was holding her. She could feel his warmth. She sighed and turned into the corner of the couch.

A hand touched her shoulder bringing her slowly awake to see the object of her dreams.

"Good morning." He said.

"Hi."

"Hungry?"

She saw the tray he had brought — all her favorites — orange juice, toast, bacon, eggs, and coffee. It brought back memories of her first meal, the first time. "No broth?" She asked with a smile as she reached for the coffee.

He smiled. "No. Now sit up and eat this before it grows cold."

Katie threw back the covers and swung her feet around. She felt the blood rush back into her ankle as she sat up. A flash of pain shot through her. She put her feet back on the couch. Chase set the tray on the coffee table and came to her aid. He gently lifted her bad ankle and placed it on the pillow.

"Looks pretty sore. How does it feel?"

"Pretty sore. Thanks." Katie said as he put her breakfast tray on her lap. He sat across from her as she began to eat. Memories continued to flood her and she let them. She remembered her pain, her feelings and how she had fled.

And here she was again. Hurt and dependent. She finished her coffee and toast fighting embarrassment. She looked and found Chase staring out the window, lost in thoughts of his own. She wondered if he too was remembering. He caught her staring.

"Remembering?"

"Yeah."

Katie waited, but he offered no more. "Can I have another cup of coffee?"

He smiled then. "Sure. Anything else?"

"Well." She hesitated. Her ankle was really beginning to throb. "Some aspirin and ice?"

He frowned as he took her tray away. Patience, she cautioned herself. You can't react to every look.

He returned with ice and a towel. "Here. You want me to put this on?"

She didn't really, but he seemed to want to. "Okay." She caught the wince but couldn't hide it when the ice touched her ankle.

"It's about as big as an apple and all purple. A real beauty. We should go in to have it looked at."

"Take me in?"

"To the hospital in Medford, remember? And have it x-rayed."

She almost spit her coffee out. The last thing she wanted to do was go anywhere. "How?" Was all she could manage to say.

"Last fall, you were a lot worse off, remember? Last fall we had snow, remember? I couldn't take you anywhere, and I couldn't leave you alone right away. There's no snow now. It's August. We can get out of here anytime we want. Unless you want to go now I suggest you sit back and see what happens here. Give me your mug and I'll get you a refill."

She quietly obeyed. After returning with her coffee and aspirin he again sat across from her. She sipped her coffee while the silence lengthened.

There was a lot that needed to be said. There were a thousand questions to ask, but she waited. She wasn't sure she was ready to hear what he had to say. She had taken an enormous risk returning, so she let the silence stretch. She couldn't go anywhere today. She would rest and let whatever was going on between them simmer for a while before giving voice to them. And given the condition of her ankle he would probably take her into Medford, whether she liked it or not. She was afraid if she left again so quickly, she wouldn't return and she wanted to be here. Finally, he broke the silence. "You will need to spend the day on the couch, and we'll keep an eye on that ankle. See if we can't get you up and around tomorrow. I've got some work to do outside, would you like more coffee before I go?"

"Yes, please."

"Okay." He smiled and his face lightened as if he pushed

whatever had been bothering him aside. Katie returned his smile. He took her mug and left.

"Thanks." She said as he brought her back pack and coffee.

"Settled? Good." He didn't wait for her response as he turned away. "I'll be in later."

"Okay." She called as the door slammed shut. Fine. She pulled out her book and began to read. But found herself wondering what Chase had been thinking about a few minutes ago. Clearly, he had been about to say something, then thought better of it. She put her book and notebook onto the floor, she wouldn't remember anything she read today anyway. The ice on her ankle had melted so she removed the towel. Then she slid down and closed her eyes to think. Sleep overtook her almost at once.

"I don't know why I'm so tired," Katie said later when Chase returned.

"You had a hard day yesterday, it's okay. Remember how much you slept last year? What you're dealing with is minor to that. So, give yourself a break and rest today."

Chase retreated to his desk, to work and to ignore her. But it was difficult to concentrate. He had worked so hard to get past the longing of the last year. He still was surprised at how much he missed her when she was gone last fall. He was once again surprised at how really happy he was to see her. That she had come back. Yet, he had been alone so long. Had worked so hard at his life the way it was, he wasn't sure if he was prepared to change. But more importantly, he wasn't sure if he gave into what he was feeling, he would survive when she left. And she would probably leave.

Finally, the years of discipline took over and he forgot about Katie and the time.

Katie observed him at work throughout the afternoon. He was so intense. He would read, stop and stare ahead all the while stroking his chin or running his hand through his hair. Then he would bend over it again and she could see him make a note in the book and then take a sheet of paper and write something down. He took a fresh sheet for every stop. She was intrigued. She wanted to know what he was reading and writing. But she didn't ask and she didn't disturb him even though the evening shadows were long, the dinner hour was long past and she was hungry.

"Why didn't you tell me it was so late?" He said suddenly, leaving his desk.

Katie jumped in surprise. "Because you were working with such concentration I didn't want to bother you."

He shook his head and frowned. He came to her, running a hand through already tousled hair. "I'm sorry." He said, "I forgot you. Don't let me do that."

He reached out his hand to help her up. "Come on. Let's go see what we can put together for dinner."

"Sure."

He moved to put his arm around her but she brushed him off. "I can do it." She said. But at her first wince of pain, he was there.

"Please."

"Okay."

She felt the strength and warmth of him. She leaned into him and as they made their way to the kitchen they exchanged a memory smile. Neither spoke until they felt Jake push his way past them breaking the moment.

"I guess she's hungry too." Chase said lightly.

After a simple meal, Chase helped her get settled in for the evening. Instead of staying with her, he went back to his desk.

Katie didn't have much energy left, and found herself glancing over at Chase as he worked. She wondered how he could be so disciplined and unaware of her presence. He looked up just then and caught her staring at him. She was surprised to see as much longing in his eyes as she felt. She looked away, back to her book or whatever.

"I'm sorry." He said softly.

Katie's head snapped up. "What?"

He came around from behind his desk and sat down across from her. "I'm sorry I've ignored you today."

"Do you drive yourself like this all the time or just when I'm here?" She was tired and gave voice to her observation.

"I don't drive myself. I've got a lot of responsibilities and there is always a lot that needs to be done."

"I see. You've been doing it so long you don't even know it."

"Doing what?"

"Driving yourself, running." She decided to push him, see what happened.

"I'm not running."

"Could have fooled me."

"You're an expert?"

"I've had some experience." She could have said more, but felt she had probably gone too far as it was. She laid down her book. "I think I'll go for a walk."

"It's dark out, and raining, besides, you can't." He settled into his chair. "Tell me about this experience you've had with running."

She looked out the window, focusing on how the rain drops hit the panes and then slowly dribbled down. Tell him about her experience with running? With being driven? That was a long story, one she'd like to tell, but with the way things were it would be too much, too soon. She was angry with him. She was angry she was angry. She wasn't about to pour her heart out now. She needed something from him first.

He was waiting. He could see the anger in her. He was curious. "Did your experience with running begin last fall or before?" He asked quietly.

"My experience at being driven began long ago. My experience at running began last fall." There she said it.

"Well," he paused, choosing his words carefully. "The experience I've had with running has taught me you can never run far enough. You either learn to deal with it or you don't."

"Well, I guess I don't have as much as experience as you.

For just when I think I've learned to live with it, I'm surprised and..." Her voice trailed away, the anger gone.

"You start running again." He finished for her.

"Yeah." She couldn't meet his eyes. She opened her book, staring all the while her eyes blurred with unshed tears.

It was a small place, this cabin in the mountains. No one could run far. He didn't want her to run anymore, but he wasn't sure he could ask her to stay and even if he did, would she stay forever? He was experienced at running. But if he gave in to the stirrings in his heart, he wouldn't be able to run far enough when she left. And so, he left her, with tears in her eyes, head in a book.

#

The next morning Chase woke first. He decided that today they would deal with practical matters. He was going to check her ankle, drive her into Medford to the clinic and have it taken care of. He knew if it didn't heal properly it would hurt her the rest of her life. He also needed a few more groceries, so that would take care of most of the day.

He quietly let Jake out and went to the kitchen to make Katie a pot of coffee. While he waited for it to brew he tried to sort out what he wanted to accomplish today, with Katie. Filling two mugs, he decided to focus on the immediate situation, getting Katie to agree to go to Medford, assuring her she could come back but he also needed an idea of what her plans really were.

Katie was aware of his presence before she opened her eyes. She heard him and could smell the fresh coffee. She wondered what the day would bring as she moved to swing her legs down and sit up. A sharp pain quickly reminded her of the situation.

"Good morning," Chase said and handed her coffee while setting his mug down on the table beside her. "Let's have a look at that ankle."

He pushed aside the blankets and gingerly touched it. He could feel Katie's wince of pain. Now was the time to put his plans for the day in motion.

"I think we're going to have to take you to the hospital and have that looked at," he said. "The swelling hasn't gone down and I am concerned about it healing properly. What do you think?"

Katie's first response was frustrating anger and she didn't look at him while she sorted through her emotions. She didn't want to leave. She didn't know if she would come back, she knew she could finish the work she brought with her anywhere. But she also knew that was just an excuse, if she got the work done, fine. If not, fine. She had time to do it when she got home. Bottom line, she was afraid. But she also knew he was right. Her ankle was really bad.

"I need to go into town anyway to get some supplies and groceries. We can do both and make a day of it."

She got the message. They would come back here afterward.

"Okay," she said. "When do you want to go?"

"After breakfast. Would you like to freshen up while I make breakfast?"

"That would be great."

He pulled her gently up to him. For a moment, she leaned into him. "Thanks, Chase," she said quietly. They both knew what she was thanking him for and he held her for a fraction longer.

18

Eighteen

Just as he had last fall, Chase helped Katie out of the cabin, only this time she could hardly walk and really had to depend on him. They went around to the back where he kept his Jeep. At her expression, he told her, "I can drive on the road as long as it hasn't rained or snowed. Last fall it had snowed and the road was impassable. It is a low or no maintenance road. Remember, when we took the four-wheelers down it?"

She remembered all too clearly the day they had left the cabin and all the events that had unfolded. But she especially remembered how quickly she was gone from him and back home.

They made their way around the edge of the meadow before heading into the trees and down a steeply sloping road. They skirted another meadow and Katie recognized this was the one where she had gotten lost just a couple of days ago. After that, it was familiar to her. Soon they would be approaching where she had stashed her rental car and the rest of her belongings. This part of her plan had always been kind of fuzzy. She wasn't ever sure when she would have come back for them or how she was going to approach it. But as they began the last downhill and curve, there was nothing left for her to do but tell him about it. He would know right away, anyway, when he saw it.

"Chase, my rental car is parked off to the side at the bottom of your road. I left the rest of my things in it and we probably should stop and get it."

"Okay," was all he could manage. He pulled alongside her Ford Focus. "Where's your stuff?" he asked as he held out his hand for her keys.

"In the trunk," she said and watched him retrieve her large suitcase and book bag.

"What are your plans, exactly?" he asked, as he turned onto the forest service road that would lead them to the main highway and into Medford.

She had wondered when he would ask and she had plenty of time to frame her answer. But it was a really hard question, even though it sounded simple.

"I have a couple of weeks of vacation. My flight home is scheduled in ten days. Freshman orientation is just around the corner and I always have a role in that."

That was an answer. Now he knew how long she would be here, how much time before she left. What remained unsaid was the why. So he asked, because he needed to know, needed to hear her say what he thought she was going to say, because it mirrored what he felt. "Why," he asked quietly, seeking her with his eyes.

She held his eyes for as long as she could, not sure what she read in them. Again, the question was not unexpected.

"Last fall was an incredible experience, and changed me. But what really happened here is hazy. I felt I needed to come back." She paused and he felt her shrug, "I needed to find out if what happened was real."

There it was out there. She said it. Out loud. To him.

She turned her attention away from him, focusing on the passing scenery of the mountains. Chase was quiet as he sorted through what she had said and had not said. He reached over and covered her hand with his.

At her look, he quietly said, "I understand." He pulled his hand away and focused his attention on the curving road as he continued, "Did you rent your car at the airport? We should make arrangements to have it sent back. There's no sense in you continuing to keep it parked out here, is there?"

"No." She answered as relief flooded through her. Their course was set, at least for the next ten days, beyond that, was well, beyond then.

The rest of the ride was quiet as they turned onto Highway 140 and then to Crater Lake Highway into Medford. Each was absorbed in what had been decided. As they drove past the airport Chase laid out what his plans were for the day.

"First, I'll drop you off at the Medford Medical Clinic and go get some groceries. We can grab lunch afterward and, on our way back take care of your car. How does that sound?"

She had no argument as she was totally dependent on him until her ankle healed. After waiting for almost an hour, they called her back to see a doctor. They had her records from her visit there the previous fall.

"This is the same ankle you hurt last fall?" The doctor asked as he looked over her chart.

"Yes," she answered.

"What did you for it then?"

"Just iced it and elevated it."

"You were able to walk on it?"

"For the most part, yes."

"And now? Can you walk on it?"

"Not really. It really hurts."

"How long ago did you injure it?"

"Two days ago."

"Less than 48 hours?"

"Yes."

"I'm going to check it to see the extent of the damage. We might have to do an x-ray, I don't think it is broken, but we'll have to see."

By the time they were done with her they had manipulated, or tried to manipulate her ankle in every direction possible. They had felt it and prodded before doing an x-ray and determining it was indeed only sprained. The bad news was she had two torn ligaments, would need an ankle brace and crutches. The crutches were to help her get around until she could put her weight back on her foot. They thought maybe in a week, she could be doing that, if she continued to rest, ice and elevate it on a regular daily basis. It didn't look like she would be doing much exploring of Chase's area, at least not on foot.

Chase was waiting for her when she hobbled out on her new crutches. He wasn't surprised to see her on them but one look at her face told him she was not happy. "What's the word?" He asked as they made their way back to his Jeep.

"Sprained, torn ligaments. Almost, but not quite the worst sprain you can have. They gave me an ankle brace to wear and these crutches. They said I could stop using the crutches when my foot holds my weight, maybe a week or so. But the ankle brace will stay for a good 4-6 weeks, depending on how strong it gets. They gave me a set of exercises to use once it starts to feel better. Did you get everything you needed?"

"Yes." He answered. "I know of a great little coffee shop we could go to for lunch, how does that sound?"

"That would be wonderful."

"I brought my lap-top, there is internet there. I need to check emails. Do you want to bring yours?"

Surprised, she simply nodded. The internet and e-mail were not new and she relied on it heavily at work, but somehow her image of Chase didn't include him utilizing technology. And it made her wonder why he didn't try to find her after last fall. She was listed on the college web site. All he had to do was google her name and he would have found her. It was enough of a question, on top of her doctor visit, to make her wonder if she really had made a good choice.

At the coffee shop, she was again surprised. It was a small shop, with tables and chairs in a large out-door garden setting. It was quiet, beautiful and busy. It was her favorite kind of place. Chase helped prop her foot on an extra chair and brought her a menu. He was gracious and kind and she was deeply grateful.

She hadn't planned to, because she didn't think she would have the chance to, but she sent John a long e-mail explaining the situation. There were a few work-related e-mails and one from Steve, informing her that he had been offered a promotion and was considering transferring to the Twin Cities in the fall. She frowned, not sure what to make of his announcement.

"Everything okay?" Chase asked, catching her look.

"Yeah," she replied logging off. "A friend of mine is thinking about moving."

"A good friend?"

"A pretty good friend. He has been offered a promotion, to supervise a larger office, so it sounds like a good career move. You have any big news?"

"No, not really. Just more details from my agent about a series of lectures I am preparing for in the fall," he paused. "You do know that I am a writer," he asked. There was so much they didn't know about each other, so much to learn.

"Yes," she said with a smile, "I did. It would be pretty hard to miss that detail. Even if I didn't see your new book in stores this summer."

"You have my new book?" He asked. "Have you read it?"

"Yes, I did. It was very interesting." She paused, should she let him know now that she had read all his other books and taught them as well. Why not? This seemed the day for laying things out on the table. But she didn't think she would tell him, yet, about her writing. "I like how it builds on the other books you have written."

At his startled look, she added, "One of the courses I teach is contemporary affairs and I use your first book in that class. I've read all of your books."

"All of them? Really?"

"Yes."

"I don't know a lot of people personally who've done that." He considered her thoughtfully.

"Are you ready to go?" He moved to gather up their things and closed up his computer.

"Yes," was her simple answer, "this was perfect."

The day in town was not over until they had navigated the traffic at the airport and made arrangements to have her rental car picked up. Their course for the next ten days, at least was set. Without a lot of additional conversation, Chase turned his Jeep back toward the mountains.

Despite the events of the day, Katie could feel him begin to withdraw, just when she was beginning to be brave. So she was back where she started, would this be something that would last longer than these few days? It was clear he needed time to process all that she had revealed. She was going to give him time to figure what he wanted to do and how or if she figured into his future.

#

Katie was sound asleep by the time Chase pulled the Jeep into its spot behind the cabin. He left her a minute to let Jake out of his kennel. Then he quietly opened her door and lifted her into his arms. She stirred and wrapped her arms around him tightly. He quietly but firmly removed her arms as he laid her on the couch.

She sleepily regarded him as he lifted her ankle and placed the pile of pillows underneath it. She didn't have the energy to do more than to quietly say, "Thank you, Chase, for the day."

"You're welcome." He said as he leaned over her and quickly touched his lips to hers. It was just a taste, but she could feel it all the way to her toes. She started to move to pull him to her, but he lifted her arms away, "Good night, Katie," he said. "I'm sure you will feel better in the morning."

When he came back after unloading groceries she was asleep did not hear him say, "Thank you, Katie, for the day."

Chase stuck to his resolve and the next day set up a pattern. He brought her book bag and lap top and set it up on the kitchen table. She could work in there while he worked at his desk.

With her crutches, Katie was a little more self-sufficient and he gave her space in the morning. He was already going out the door when she stirred. "I've got some chores to do outside," he said. "There is coffee in the kitchen, make yourself at home."

She contemplated the situation and the events of the day before while sipping her first cup of coffee of the day. She wasn't stupid, she could feel Chase pulling away, perhaps she had revealed too much, but it couldn't be undone now. She would give him the space he needed, hoping he would come back to her. She wanted to fight for him, but she wasn't going to throw herself at him. She was here, after all. He had to choose. There was a little over a week left before she had to leave, plenty of time to sort things out. She brought out her book bag, sorted through her things and made a to-do list. She had come prepared.

Several days later she wondered how much space Chase really needed. The routine included him leaving the cabin each morning to do chores. He had a small garden he tended and he cut firewood and stacked it under the lean-to behind the cabin, beside his Jeep.

Katie would work at the kitchen table, make lunch for them and clean up. In the afternoons, Chase would work at his desk while Katie hobbled outside to sit in the warm afternoon sun soaking up the scenery and quiet. She had Chase help bring out her bag with a book, paper and sometimes her lap top. Sometimes she worked, sometimes she just sat until she nodded off, and trying not to think about how painful it would be to leave again.

She didn't know if she would recover from leaving again, but she now had some advice from an expert runner. Learn to live with it, he said. She wondered how he did it. She didn't know if she could. But, of course she could and would. Besides, her experience of the last year had taught her a lot. If things didn't change, she would leave and never look back.

In the late afternoon, they would spend time together. Chase would come out and help her bring her things in, and then they would settle in the kitchen while Chase made dinner. This was her favorite time of the day. The first couple of days after their trip into Medford, they had by tacit agreement avoided any subjects that brought them too close to themselves. For the most part, these conversations allowed them to get to know each other better, but once in a while they strayed too close to their situation and the time quickly ended.

One evening, Katie asked him about his garden and through that conversation revealed her own love of gardening. While he grew his for immediate consumption, she grew hers for eating and freezing. This was something Chase had always wanted to do, but was limited by his living situation. So he was very interested in hearing how much she grew and how she preserved it for the winter. His curiosity prompted him to ask, without thinking, "Isn't this the time to do that?"

"Normally, but the last two years I planted my garden purposefully late. When I get home it should be ready." She didn't mention that last year, she had let it go to waste as she didn't have the energy to deal with it. But they were both reminded again that she would leave in a few short days and silence lengthened the meal.

After dinner, Chase would help her outside again and they would quietly enjoy watching the shadows grow long and deep over Chase's meadow as the sun set in the west. It was at this time Chase told her about his family, the one sister he was very close to who still lived near their childhood home in Cooperstown, NY. This bit of information prompted Katie to ask about baseball and to learn that he loved baseball, and played it in high school and that he was a Yankee's fan.

Another evening, they talked about their college careers. She learned that he had gone to Cornell University, worked for former U.S. Senator Daniel Patrick Moynihan before going to UVA law school.

Katie was jealous of his background. She had only been able to afford to go to Mankato State University and then obtained her Masters from the University of Minnesota. As a history major and teacher, she could only wonder at what it would have been like to go to school amidst the rich history of Virginia and Thomas Jefferson's legacy.

Under this routine, Katie finished reading the books she had brought and started working on her writing project. One morning she lost track of time and forgot to make lunch. She was startled when Chase came in looking for something to eat.

Katie looked up surprised. Why wasn't he working? What did he want?

"What are you doing?" He asked.

"I'm working on a writing project. It's a part of what I do."

"You finished reading all the books you brought?"

"I only had a couple and they were pretty easy reads."

He had expressed only a passing interest in what she had been working on. She knew what he was doing, he had kind of told her that when they were in Medford and she knew the routine he established was something that would work for her, given what she had brought along in her book bag and back pack. But still he really, didn't know what she had been doing every morning. He simply left her alone while he worked. Neither one had pressed beyond the moment about anything.

"It's lunch time. I'd say whatever you're working on must be pretty intense. You don't normally lose track of time. No," he said, as she started to get up. "I'll get lunch today. Don't let me distract you."

Katie almost snorted at that, did he not realize his effect on her? There was a reason she worked in the kitchen while he worked in the living room. He was the one who set up the situation and given how he had stuck to his routine, she simply followed. Now here he was, telling her he hoped he wouldn't distract her.

"That's all right," she said, stacking her papers beside her lap top. "I could use a break."

"What are you working on so intently?" He asked again. "Soup, okay?"

When she still didn't answer, he said, "You don't have to tell me, if you don't want to. I was just curious, that's all."

"It's just a project I've committed to," she answered, her frustration and patience quickly boiling over.

"You know," she said quietly, "I don't know what you want. I came back here because I needed to, and you encouraged me to stay. But you threw up these walls, this schedule and routine. I really don't know what I am doing here anymore. I'm not really hungry, I'm going outside." With that Katie packed up her stuff and went out the front door.

She was right. She had told him why she came back and she knew why he had agreed to let her stay. If only he would be honest with himself, she thought, he would admit that he enjoyed her company and the camaraderie of being able to work separately but together. But he had kept his distance, hadn't touched her again, since coming back from Medford. But each evening it was getting harder. Things weren't any different at this moment than they were the first day she arrived. Now if he didn't figure things out, she would leave for good.

19

Nineteen

By the next morning, Chase had reached a new decision. The cabin was just too small for the both of them. Despite everything, he just couldn't consider his future or theirs, while being under the same roof all the time. Problem was, his life was so scattered, and he didn't know how she could or would fit into his future. Routines were all fine and good, but they only provided so much protection. He needed time alone, in a place where he wouldn't stumble over her at every turn. He wasn't sure what her response would be, he was only sure she couldn't leave until he returned. While she was walking some, she didn't have the stamina to hike out and he trusted she wouldn't take the Jeep.

He quietly put together things, a change of clothes, his sleeping bag, a notebook and his folder for his lectures into his well-used back pack. He would go up the mountain to a place where he could quietly consider what his options might be.

Katie found him putting together food supplies when she came into the kitchen for her first cup of coffee. Her heart sank. “You’re leaving?” She asked.

“Look, I’m going up the mountain for a couple of days. I’m leaving Jake with you. You can sleep in the bed.” He turned back to her, holding her eyes to his.

He went to her, took her face in his hands and kissed her gently and then held her close. “I’m sorry. I know you’re disappointed and hurt. You aren’t wrong, but I need some time alone to think and sort things out. We’ll talk when I get back. We have time before you have to leave. Okay?” He whispered in her ear before releasing her.

She could only nod her head.

“Katie, I’m glad you took a chance on me and came back. I really am. I don’t want you to leave. Please stay until I come back.”

“I will.”

“Goodbye then.” He left.

“Goodbye.” She whispered to the empty room.

Jake whined in the living room. She went to him. His large eyes were sad and he wagged his tail forlornly. She patted the seat next to her and he jumped right up, laying his head in her lap. “I know.” She said. “He left us. But he’ll be back. He said he would. And we’re supposed to stay here and you’re supposed to take care of me and I’m supposed to take care of you.”

Jake seemed satisfied with that and closed his eyes. Yes, she thought. He loves Jake. But what does he feel for me? What is he going to do? Where is he going? What happens when he gets back? What is he going to decide? How will I feel? Why do I have to stay here and wait? Wait for what? The questions and uncertainties chased through her mind over and over again until she was bone weary from it all. Pushing Jake unto the floor she curled around her pillow and willed the memory of Chase as he left, Chase with tenderness in his eyes for her, Chase who wanted her to wait, Chase who was glad to see her, Chase who she loved more than she cared to admit. Memories soothed her, comforted her and she slept.

She woke feeling calmer and more refreshed than she had in a long time. She and Jake went outside and soaked up the late afternoon sun. She let her thoughts wander with her eyes.

It was a beautiful sight. The hills and ridges down to the valley were a carpet of lush green. The sun highlighted the top and the shadows were dark and deep. Last fall this view was quite different. Then it had been filled with the hint of the golds, rusts and browns of fall. And every much as beautiful as it appeared today.

A lot has changed since then, she thought. Not only the seasons. I've changed. Chase has changed. Yet, she thought hard, something has remained. Despite his distance and her bruised emotions being here in these mountains, in this cabin, with him. She still felt a strong sense of peace. She knew she still thought too much, that she didn't trust her emotions. That's what Steve had always told her.

Steve. She wondered how he was. He was not happy with her decision to come here. She wondered if he would be there when she returned. She had been painfully honest with him. There should be no surprises when she got back.

Katie took a deep breath pushing the thoughts away. "Come on Jake." She called. The black lab came running and Katie could read the question in his eyes. "Sorry. Remember? You're supposed to take care of me. I'll take care of you. I promised."

Jake didn't seem to be reassured. He was all hangey-dog. They went into the cabin as the sun set over the ridge, casting long shadows over the valley. It was quiet, she was relaxed, and surprised she was actually glad to have the place to herself. The tension had been so high between them, it seemed like a load had been lifted from her shoulders.

She stood taking it all in. Her backpack had been left in the bedroom. The pillows and blankets she used were stacked on the bed. He had moved everything for her. It would feel good to sleep in a bed again, she thought. Real good. But she wasn't ready for sleep yet.

#

Later, much later, she nearly jumped out of her chair when a loud thunder clap shook the cabin. Jake stirred at her feet, growled and his hair stood up. Katie had been so involved with her project she had barely noticed when darkness blanketed the cabin. The only light on was over the table in the kitchen where she was working.

The cabin had grown chilly as the front worked its way

across the valley. Katie went and pulled on a sweatshirt. Then stood at the front window, in the dark, watching the lightening display the mountain peaks shrouded in thunder clouds. Jake stood with her quivering and growling. "Shh." Katie said. "It's just a storm." Another flash of lightening lit up the cabin and Jake ran to the front door in a panic.

"Jake. Come." Katie moved away from the window and turned on a light. Sitting on the floor by the couch, she called again to the dog. He came then and he had an unfamiliar, scared look in his eyes. She thought it strange he would be so afraid, although she knew some dogs were. She wasn't used to it. Misty didn't get scared of storms. In fact, it seemed that Misty actually enjoyed them.

Jake quieted down some and when the next lightning bolt struck, she held him firm. The thunder rolled but she wouldn't let him up. "Shh." She soothed as she stroked him over and over. "Shh." He quieted and relaxed finally, closing his eyes against the storm.

He was sleeping on her lap. She was stuck at least until the storm quieted down. Close at hand was an end table with rather large books stacked underneath. She had never noticed them before. She reached out and was pleasantly surprised to find a stack of Chase's old year books.

Eagerly, Katie turned the pages, starting with the earliest year. She paged through one and then another as the storm flashed and thundered about outside. She didn't notice, until her legs fell asleep under the weight of Jake. Gently she eased herself out from underneath and decided to read the rest of the books in bed. A luxury she hadn't enjoyed for some time.

Every light was extinguished save one as Katie settled comfortably in bed. She continued to search the yearbooks for clues to Chase's past. There weren't many pictures and the ones that were there hardly resembled him. He was thin and scraggly, invariably with a beard or unshaven. But his eyes were the same. They were the same dark pools that she had lost herself in. She remembered Steve's comment on Chase and women. Yes, she could see it. He was the lost soul who needed rescuing. She hoped he didn't view her as another one trying to rescue him from himself. Although, she thought dryly, he did need rescuing.

A crash of thunder brought her back to the present. The clock on the bed stand said 12:00, time for sleep. She closed the books and snuggled down under the covers.

Thunder and lightning still rumbled about, but the storm had lost its strength. Rain now fell in a steady stream, causing a quiet drumming on the roof. Katie missed Chase in that moment. But she would wait, as she promised.

#

When Katie woke in the gray light of dawn, she didn't know where she was. It took her a moment to remember she was in Chase's bed, in Chase's cabin but Chase was gone. She could hear the steady pitter patter of the rain on the roof and felt the chill of the cabin. She pushed herself deeper under the covers in an effort to go back to sleep. It was futile.

She laid with her eyes closed, listening to the rain, thinking about the day that stretched ahead of her, a quiet, lonely, rainy day. She had had plenty of those kinds of days, she knew how to fill them. She just had to get started.

Jake's wet nose pressed against her cheek was just what she needed. "Good morning, Jake." She said, "Do you want to come?" In a moment, Jake was cuddled against her, but he didn't stay. Bounding out of bed he went to the door. "You want to go out?"

She got out of bed and looked out into the steady downpour. "I know. But you might have to stay out in your dog house the rest of the day," she said as she let him out the door.

Within minutes, she heard him back at the door. She let him in with a firm command, "stay." She got a dirty towel and dried him off as best she could and then commanded him to follow her to the kitchen where she got a pot of coffee going. She gave Jake his food and then returned to the living room to build a fire to take the cool edge off the day. If I keep myself busy, she reminded herself as she cleaned up after Jake's wet foot prints, the day will go a lot faster.

Returning to the kitchen she poured herself a cup of coffee and then proceeded to fix herself a huge breakfast of bacon, eggs, and toast. She was starving as she realized she had forgotten to eat dinner the night before.

It wasn't until she sat down to eat that she looked out the window overlooking the valley. It was awash with little rivers of water digging ever deeper into the hillside. Everything was wet and the mud was very deep. It was still raining very steady and did not look like it would be letting up soon. She assumed that Chase was safe. She also assumed he would not be back today, maybe not even tomorrow. It was so wet and muddy the trails wouldn't be safe.

She finished eating and cleaned up her dishes. Pouring another cup of coffee, she sat at the table, staring out the window, contemplating her day. Jake nestled close and she absently stroked his head. She knew she needed to get moving before her emotions took control. Yet, she wanted to baby herself a little bit more. She let the feelings of longing and hope charge around a bit, before burying them again. She thought of Chase's last words, his last look. It was so full of promise. She focused on that.

Feeling a little better, she took her coffee into the bathroom and began running a hot bath. She had the privacy she needed to indulge herself a bit. Jake went back to the front door, whining to be let out. "Okay," she said as she let him out, "but you may need a bath when you come back."

The hot bath did the trick. The peace of being here stayed with her. She knew she was in the right place. Chase knew why she was here. He needed to decide, and soon.

With that decided she felt determined and full of energy. Since she couldn't go outside she decided to work off her energy inside by cleaning. The cabin looked lived in, well used, but messy. She would straighten things up.

At lunch time she made a sandwich and ate it with a glass of milk at the kitchen table. The rain continued to fall outside the window. Everything was soaked. Water was standing in the low areas. She wondered if it cooled off more if it would snow. That would be fitting, she thought. But she'd rather Chase was back before the weather got any worse. She hoped he was safe and dry. She didn't want to contemplate the notion that he was anything but safe and dry.

It was time to begin the living room. First, she dusted the end tables, moving piles of books and magazines. The bookshelves commanded her attention next. They were large, filling the whole wall from floor to ceiling. And they were filled. She had become familiar with their contents last fall, but this year she had not had the need to find something to do. She had brought it all with her. She contemplated removing all the books to give the shelves a thorough dusting. But her urge to go the extra mile was gone. Instead, she carefully dusted each of the shelves. As she did she read the titles once again. There many law books, but she was surprised at the number of books on philosophy and theology. She shouldn't have, all his books were heavy on philosophy. Nevertheless, she was amazed at the range of works he had studied.

She found copies of his own books, including the new one, Contemporary Affairs. She hadn't looked at it since she had finished it shortly after her return from New York. She pulled it from the shelf and sat down to page through it. Immediately, the dedication caught her attention. It continued to puzzle her, "To Kaycee," she read. Who was Kaycee? Then she slammed the cover shut. She wasn't going to let anything ruin her good spirits.

As she replaced it, she remembered seeing a book of her poems tucked in with the other books last fall. She hadn't noticed it today. Maybe she missed it. She carefully looked over each shelf. Nope. It was gone.

Finishing her job, she looked around the room. For a long time, she contemplated his work area. She was just dying to get a glimpse into what he was working on, but finally decided it was best to leave things alone.

Returning to the kitchen she was surprised to see the time. It was after 4:00 pm. No wonder she felt tired, she had been cleaning most of the day! Brewing a fresh pot of coffee, she searched through the refrigerator for something to make for dinner. Finding the left-over spaghetti, she took a close look and decided it was still okay to eat. Dinner solved.

Her books and notebooks were still piled on the kitchen table from the day before. Having taken the day off gave her some freshness to begin writing again. She worked until the gray light of day had turned dark. The rain had stopped. In fact, she could see the faint light of the setting sun around the edges of the clouds. Maybe tomorrow the sky would be clear and the warm sun would dry the soaked ground and maybe then Chase will be back.

It was then she remembered Jake was still outside and hadn't even come to the door knocking. She flew to the door. "Jake." She called. "Jake. Come. Jake." She waited. He didn't come.

"Jake. Come." She called in as a commanding voice as she could muster. "Jake."

She waited, still nothing, but darkness was falling quickly. Maybe he's sleeping in his dog house and didn't hear me, she thought. In reality she didn't think it likely, but she didn't want to consider that Jake was gone. Maybe he had just gone for a walk, dogs were known to do that, she reminded herself. No need to panic.

With darkness came the coolness of night. Katie stoked the fire as she pondered what to do about the missing Jake. He generally was an obedient dog. If he heard her calling he would come. It he didn't then he wasn't close enough for her to even find him even if she went looking. She stood at the window, staring out into the darkness. No moon. No shadows. It was nearly pitch dark, with a wet and muddy ground. Not optimum searching conditions.

A few rain drops hit the window pane. It was raining again, a soft gentle rain. Lightening flashed across the valley and for a moment she could see the mountains framed in clouds, then blackness. The thunder was faint.

It was the thunder and lightning that decided it for her. Jake was scared of storms. She needed to make the effort to find him.

She just needed her rain jacket and some boots. The rain jacket was easy. Finding a pair of rain boots in Chase's closet was another story.

In the kitchen she grabbed the flash light from its spot on the counter. She pulled on her tennis shoes, her rain jacket and stepped into the dark, dark night. She circled around the cabin calling, "Jake. Jake." No response. She checked his dog house, empty. She limped across the meadow, careful to keep the cabin in the light of her flashlight.

"Jake. Jake." She called. Only silence responded. She knew then that it was futile. She couldn't begin to imagine where he was. She didn't know his haunts. She could only hope he was safe.

Nevertheless, it was with a sinking heart that she returned to the cabin. She was muddy, wet, cold and discouraged. Her ankle again pounded in pain.

The second warm bath of the day, her flannel pj's and warm socks soothed her spirits but didn't replace the sense of loneliness of the silent cabin. The warmth of the fire beckoned, but she ignored it and crawled into the empty bed. Jake was gone. Chase was gone. She had been so stupid, to come all this way and then to pull back the first time she got scared.

She needed someone who needed her, but at the same time was stronger than her. Chase was strong, that was what drew her to him. He was determined, objective and smart. But he overwhelmed and intimidated her. And he didn't seem to need anyone. She kept her walls up when what she wanted most was for him to know her, admire her and like her too. No, love her too. She was almost out of time, but not quite. He asked her to wait. He told her he needed to sort out things. So, she would wait.

Her pillow was wet when she finally went to sleep.

20

Twenty

In the middle of the night a scratching noise woke her. She heard the sound of the rain on the roof then she heard the sound again. Someone was at the door. Jake!

She ran and opened the door. Chase stumbled in, followed by Jake. They were both soaking wet. Although she couldn't see Chase's face, she could tell something was wrong.

"Katie." He whispered and she caught him as he fell. Jake whimpered as she half carried him to the couch. Once she got him down she pulled off his rain-soaked jacket. He was wet to the bone. He was shivering uncontrollably and his lips were blue. She had to get his clothes off. She had to get him warm. Jake was running around them whimpering, and in the way.

"Lay down," Katie commanded the dog. She threw more wood on the fire, and then she quickly got towels and quilts and blankets off the bed. Returning to Chase, she fumbled as she undid his shoes and removed his socks. Next was his shirt, then his jeans. She needed to get him wrapped in the blankets, but she needed his help.

"Chase, Chase. Wake up. Help me, Chase."

"Warm, Katie, I need warm," he moaned.

"Yes, I know. Help me Chase."

He leaned into her and together they fell to the floor. She wrapped him like a mummy in the blankets. He opened his eyes and urged her, "Something warm to drink, please, Katie. But not coffee." She saw a ghost of a smile before he fell silent against her.

"Shh," She said. "I'll get it. Rest. Don't worry I'll take care of you."

As she left his side, Jake came over and snuggled up against him. "Good dog, Jake," she said. "Good dog."

In the kitchen, Katie focused on making hot water while searching the cupboards for dried soup or tea. She wasn't sure if Chase was seriously hurt or just cold to the bone from the rain. Whatever, she knew her first priority was to get him warm.

Returning, she found him out and the blue tint had returned to his lips. She lifted him against her. "Chase. Chase. Wake up. Come on, wake up." His eyes flickered open and he tried to sit up. Katie lifted him against her and held the cup to his lips. Ever so slowly she helped him until the whole cup was gone. Then she laid him down again, considering her next step. His lips were no longer blue, but she was still concerned. She folded back the blanket and felt his skin. He was still cold, so cold. His breathing was so shallow.

She maybe did stupid things like backpack into the mountains wearing tennis shoes, but she did know now that he was on the verge of hypothermia. If she didn't get him warm soon, he could go into cardiac arrest. Immediate medical attention was not an option right now. She was it.

Quickly, she drew back the blankets and lay with him, skin to skin. She pulled the blankets up around them, making sure to cover Chase's head. Jake lay down next to Chase on the other side and she could feel his warmth through the blankets. "Good dog," she said.

As she settled herself against him, she could feel the soft, slow beat of his heart. He draped an arm around her and pulled her tightly against him. Otherwise, he didn't stir. He was so cold. All she could do now was hope and pray. She closed her eyes and relaxed.

She must have fallen asleep because she was suddenly surprised to notice the fire was low. There was a chill in the air. Then she realized she was lying wrapped in blankets with Chase. She listened to his breathing. Normal. Thank God, she thought as she moved to ease out from under Chase's arm and out of the blankets. He was warm. He was normal.

"Don't leave. Please." Chase whispered and held her.

"I won't."

He released her, but she made no move to leave the cocoon of blankets.

"You probably saved my life."

"You saved mine. It's only fair I save yours. Now we're even."

"Is that why you came back?"

"What?"

"You came back to me." He wanted to hear her say it. He wanted to know.

She remained silent.

"You told me you needed to come back." He began to gently caress her shoulder, letting his hand wander as his eyes held hers, gently, but firmly pulling her close. "But you weren't very specific. Tell me, please. I want to know."

"Yes." She was aware of everywhere their bodies touched. "I came back because I wanted to know if what I felt was real or something I just imagined." His lips claimed hers.

"Is it?" He asked between kisses, their breath mingling.

"I don't know. You tell me."

"Why?" He asked again. They broke apart as he waited and she debated. He watched the emotions shift through her eyes.

"I couldn't forget."

"Couldn't forget? What?"

"You."

"Why couldn't you forget me?" He whispered. "I really do want to know. I want to understand."

"Well, last fall I wasn't myself here, with you. I was hurt. I felt vulnerable and scared."

"Scared?"

"I was scared of you. You intimidated me. I was attracted

to you. I was hurt. I wasn't myself. I wasn't sure of what was going on. I questioned everything."

"So when the chance came to leave, you left."

"Well," she paused for significance. "You didn't stop me."

"But you decided to come back now."

"Yes. I haven't functioned well since I left," her voice trailed off. She was not going to tell him just how dysfunctional she had been. How she had slept poorly, ate poorly and drove herself to forget something she finally realized she couldn't forget until she knew.

Now she knew. And he would know too. It was the only way to find out.

"Well," he said. "I haven't exactly had the greatest year either."

His admission was a start in the right direction, she thought.

"How long are you, can you stay?"

"Just a couple of more days."

"And then?"

"And then I have to get back."

"Exactly where is back?"

She smiled then. "You didn't know?"

"Not exactly. By the time I wanted to find you, I realized I only knew your name, but didn't know where in Minnesota you lived. I knew you were a teacher, but not what or where. And I couldn't get any details from the hospital. Data privacy, you know."

She wanted to ask him why he didn't google her name,

but decided to simply answer his question. "I live in St. Peter Minnesota. I teach at a small college there. I have to get back to begin the fall semester. School starts right after Labor Day. There are workshops, faculty meetings, freshmen orientation, all that. I also have an October 1st deadline for the stuff I've been working on while I've been here. I haven't been under contract before for my writing, so I'm a little nervous about it."

"You've never been under deadline before?"

"No. Before I just worked and when I could get it published I did. This time though I was organized enough to make a pitch and they bought it."

"I know something of deadlines. They're rough. They're demanding." He thought of the deadlines he had been under last fall. How it had caused so much pressure he let her push him away, he let her flee. But she was back. "I'm under deadline too, October 1st, too."

"What are you working on?"

"I'm developing a lecture tour based on my new book, Contemporary Affairs. I'll be touring small colleges and universities for six weeks in October and November."

"Oh." It was the beginning of the end after all. He saw her sadness and cupped her face in his hand, forcing grey eyes to meet brown.

"I'm doing pretty well on this deadline. I have some spare time."

"Spare time?" She whispered, afraid yet hopeful.

"Spare time to spend with you." To really get to know you

and then…he didn't finish the thought as he brought her to him again. "I want to spend the time you have left here with you, starting now." He said against her lips. "How are you doing with your deadline? Do you have time?"

"Yes." How could she say anything else? This is what she wanted. This is why she came to be with him, to find out. She would deal with the end later. Now she would be happy with now. For it was all she was guaranteed.

No more words were spoken. No one left the cocoon of blankets before the dying fire. Jake stirred and moved away, but nothing disturbed Chase and Katie. They rested comfortably in the knowledge that there was a tomorrow for them.

#

It was the bright sunlight of morning and the cold nuzzle of Jake that woke Katie the second time. "Okay, pal" Katie said softly. "I'll let you out."

Slipping quietly out from the blankets and away from Chase, Katie quickly pulled on her discarded t-shirt and shorts and let the dog out. Moving quietly, she went to the kitchen to make coffee. When the coffee was finished, she tip-toed to the bathroom to shower and clean up.

What a difference twenty-four hours can make, she thought, as the hot water poured over her. She replayed the conversation and events of the night over in her mind. If she thought she was scared last fall because of her feelings, it was nothing to what she felt now. He had asked her to stay, to spend time with him, to get to know him and to be with him. It was wonderful, but what would happen when she left? She pushed that thought out of her mind and turned to the day at hand. She didn't know how Chase would feel. If he would rebound and be fine or if he was going to need a little time to recover from the close call of the night before. Which reminded her, he needed to tell her where he had been and how he got caught in the storm.

She went to where she had left him and knelt down next to him. "Chase. Chase," she said. "It's morning. You should get up and see if you can eat."

He stirred and his eyes were tired.

"How do you feel?"

"Tired, but otherwise good," he answered.

"Well, there is no reason for you to stay there on the floor. Would you like me to make you something to eat? Would you like a shower?"

"Interesting set of questions," he said as his smile changed his whole face.

"I think you are nearly normal. Come on. Get up." Katie reached out a hand to help him up. He stood, the blankets falling to the floor. But he couldn't stand without help. That became obvious fast as he almost collapsed back onto the floor.

"Here, what do you want to do?" she asked as he leaned onto her for support.

"I think a shower, a change of clothes and something to eat would be perfect," he said. "Just get me to the bedroom and I can take it from there."

It turned out to be an interesting and long day. Chase took his shower while Katie made something for them to eat. But Chase really didn't have any energy and so Katie encouraged him to spend the day in bed. "It's my turn to take care of you," she said. "You need to let me take care of you, okay?"

"That sounds like a good plan for today," he said. He grabbed her hand as she turned away. "Katie,"

She looked at him, feeling the tenderness his eyes held.

"Thanks."

"Sure." Overwhelmed, she almost fled for the kitchen, but she remembered her resolve not to run. She leaned over and kissed him lightly.

As the day progressed, it was clearly a good decision for Chase to stay off his feet. He ate almost everything she had made him for breakfast and felt sleep pulling at him. He wanted to talk to her. He had questions he wanted to ask. But mostly he just wanted to talk. He knew he loved her. But it was strange to him. It was such a natural thing yet he didn't know why.

He thought about how strange it felt to him, someone who maintained a high degree of independence. For a man who sought to understand and have an explanation for everything, it was intimidating. For a man who had thought he loved and had been burned, it was scary. But for a man who wrote about faith, it was time to practice what he preached. As his eyes closed in sleep, he thought only of her and how he could assure her that she had not returned to him in vain.

If Katie had glimpsed his thoughts, her own day would

have passed more smoothly. She knew their relationship had crossed into new ground, but she wasn't sure what it meant.

Later in the afternoon, she set aside her project. She couldn't concentrate anymore. Chase had slept quietly throughout the day. Katie woke him at noon to give him some soup. "How are you feeling?" She asked.

"Better, but still so tired."

"That is to be expected, I think."

Not much else was said while Chase finished. "I hope this is the last day of this," he said. "I can't remember the last time I slept this much. I would much rather be up, being with you."

Katie smiled. "There will be time," she said.

"Will there?" He asked. His dark brown eyes serious and his expression intent. "You won't leave right away?"

"No, Chase," she said. "But I only have a few days left."

"Good, we have things to talk about, but I can't today."

"That's okay. Today's not good for me either."

He smiled at that. As she reached for the tray, he reached up, pulled her face to his and kissed her gently. Katie's hands were holding the tray and it was all she could do not to drop it. It was a light brush, but there were sparks.

Now it was time to put pen and paper to good use. Writing was something she could do. Writing would help her make sense of everything. Why did she have to try making sense of it? Chase's words, his kiss overwhelmed her. It only made her long for more and she too looked forward to tomorrow, when, hopefully, he would be back to normal and up and around.

#

He was. He woke her the next morning with a kiss. Startled, she opened her eyes and tried to sit up. “Not yet.” He said and kissed her again. Sleepily she smiled and said, “Good morning. You’re feeling better, I see.”

“Yes. I am. Time to get going. I’ll make the coffee.”

“Okay.”

He left and she absorbed the fact that he had taken a shower. His damp hair was combed and he had trimmed his beard. His walk betrayed his fatigue.

There was no more time to waste. There was a hint of fall in the air and no matter what had been said, Katie would be leaving. She had a deadline. Chase knew from experience what that meant. Meeting a deadline was everything. You missed it, you missed out. He couldn’t figure out why sometimes she was so skittish around him, so nervous and intimidated. Ah, he thought, she is intimidated by me for some reason. But after the last couple of nights, maybe that was in the past. His thoughts were interrupted by Katie’s arrival in the kitchen.

“Coffee ready?” She asked.

“Just for you,” he said as he poured her a cup. His hand brushed hers as he handed off the cup and there were those sparks again.

“Thanks.” Katie quickly stepped away and sat at the table, looking out the window at the mountains shaded in the pale yellow of morning sunlight. Today was the day she had anticipated and looked forward to and now here it was. It felt so normal to be here. As it should, she thought.

Smiling at him, she asked, “What do you feel like doing today? Do you need to do some work? I have a little I can do to stay on schedule, but not a lot.”

“I should do a little too, but I’m not very excited about it. I would like to get some fresh air this morning and go from there. Would that work?”

“I think that sounds like the making of a good plan. Now what shall we have for breakfast?”

21

Twenty-One

The fresh air of morning invited Chase and Katie outdoors. They needed the warmth of the sun, the openness of the mountains and activity to begin the process they both desired and needed, to be together, to know one another.

The ground was still wet from the rain and the grass scrunched under their feet. Katie's tennis shoes were getting wet at the toes. She didn't know why she hadn't worn hiking boots. It was a gross oversight on her part and she wished she had them on her feet instead of in a closet in Minnesota. Her ankle felt pretty strong, but the extra support would have been reassuring. She certainly didn't want to injure it again.

Chase called for Jake and he came running across the meadow, very happy to see them. Then as suddenly as he started, Jake plopped down panting, his tongue hanging out of his mouth and slobbering. Chase laughed and Katie smiled, shook her head and said, "Silly dog."

Chase stopped laughing, "Yes, sometimes he is. But he also saved my life."

"Oh, really," Katie said. "What happened?"

"I was coming down from my spot higher up during the rain storm. It was pretty muddy. I was pretty wet. Anyway, I slipped in the mud. I must have hit my head or something. Jake found me and licked my face and nudged at me until I opened my eyes. I somehow managed to get up and," he paused. "The rest, they say is history."

She became aware again that Chase was watching her. "Where are we going?" she asked. "It is so beautiful here."

They were standing in a small meadow, surrounded by pines and towering peaks. It was remote, quiet and spectacular. "I thought I'd show you around my little meadow."

She followed him as he went around the back of the cabin to where the Jeep was parked. Here the meadow fell away to the valley below. "It does not," Chase said, "go straight down to the valley. It falls away in a series of dips and rises. There is a small stream at the bottom of this ridge. He smiled at her then, and said, "The logging road I use takes you away from the stream to the road. If you keep going from where you left your car, you will find a hiking trail. It is not always passable, but it is there. This is where it ends."

He showed her a faint trail that wound down through the bushes and rocks. "The electric lines come up through here," he said.

"I had wondered about that," Katie said. "Wasn't it difficult to get electricity up here?" She moved down the trail a few feet to where the trail fell away steeply. She came back up. "How did you get everything up here? When I was here last year, we couldn't drive out because of the weather."

They walked away from the Jeep and headed across the small meadow.

"I found the cabin when I was about 15. I was in the lower meadow, backpacking with a large group. We had our main camp there and took day hikes around the whole mountain. I often went alone, imagine that," he laughed awkwardly. Katie smiled. She already knew that.

"I came up this way one day. When you first come across the ridge, where we came," he pointed across to the far side of the meadow, "you can't see the cabin. It's camouflaged very well. But I found it. Some old mountain man built it many, many years ago. It was very dirty, but it was built solid. The bookshelves were there, plus lots of junk. I was fascinated and I began to dream of living here. I cleaned it and explored the meadow so I could find it again. As you found out, this meadow is very hard to see from the valley below. It only looks like another ridge in a series of ridges.

"I actually didn't get back here until I was twenty. It was the summer between my junior and senior year in college and I needed to get away, to sort out what I was going to do after I graduated," He paused and smiled at her. "Anyway, I found it right away. Of course, the cleaning job I had done five years before was destroyed with time. I came prepared, however and cleaned it like it had never been cleaned before.

Then I fixed it up, made it weather proof again. I chopped firewood, just in case I came back in the fall or winter. I explored some more, climbed up and found a small lake. And I searched behind the cabin and found the logging road below. I made plans, I loved this place.

"During law school, I tried to spend a month up here every summer. But I didn't move in or do any more to it. I didn't own it. Once I passed the bar and had my first job I checked into who owned this part of the mountain. I was lucky," he smiled and she could see the sense of pride he had in this place. "No one owned it. So I did the paper work, paid the government and became the owner. That was about eight years ago," he paused.

His story certainly provided a little more insight, but she knew most of it anyway. The question was, did he really thrive on being alone or was he merely playing it safe? Even most introverts needed some people in their lives. He didn't appear to need any. How could he go from not needing anyone to needing her? It appeared he did, but given his history, and his age, could he adjust to having someone else in his life? For now it seemed she had more questions and very little time for answers.

"When did you start writing," she asked.

"I started writing while I was in law school. You know, the law review and journals. After, I just kept at it, only they became books. Once I started earning money at it, or enough, I quit my job with a law firm to focus on writing.

Being a traditional lawyer was not something that really suited me."

"Why, too many people around?" She asked before she thought, immediately wishing she would have kept her mouth shut.

He looked at her for a long moment, weighing his answer. He wasn't stupid. He knew how he looked to her. He was eccentric. He maybe could explain himself, but maybe not now, not yet. "Yes, too many people," he said.

They walked the rest of the way across the meadow in silence. Katie felt the tension grow between them again. He had pulled back abruptly, closed down.

"This is the trail we came up the other day," he said pointing out a faint path at the edge of the woods. "And over here," he walked a few feet to the right, "is the trail to that little lake I told you about, where I was the other day."

Taking her hand in his he said, "I think we have explored enough for one day. We both have work to do to stay on deadline and I am actually tired." He pulled her to him gently. "We do have time," he whispered before he kissed her.

They made their way back to the cabin in silence, content for now, but aware the clock was ticking.

#

The next day found Chase and Katie outside again after breakfast. There was virtually no time left for them but today. Katie's plane ticket was for the next day. She felt she had more answers and a better sense of their relationship, yet the future remained uncertain. She couldn't stay, but he could follow.

It didn't need to be an end. This time together could be a beginning. They could make plans.

"Help me understand something," she said. "Why were you so determined to make a home here? It is beautiful, peaceful and I can certainly understand your attraction. You've done so much here. Don't you miss being around people on a regular basis, don't you get lonely?"

"You have to remember that I don't live up here all year. I spend most of my summers here, but the rest of the year it is difficult to get here and stay here. The road becomes impassable later in the fall and isn't open completely again until late spring."

"I've always admired you Chase," Katie said, honestly, "your ideas, your writing and sense of integrity. But I don't understand how you function on your own all the time. Don't you need people?"

"I need people," he said. "But I don't need to be around people. I used to, too much maybe. I've had my share of relationships. I have good friends around the country I like to see and be with. I keep up with them. Today's technology doesn't allow you to be out of touch for too long. Except here. But I just drive to town and I can be in touch if I want to. I know they are there, that they will be there for me when I need them. I don't need to be with them and doing things with them to know that. What are you looking for?"

"I don't know, maybe I'm trying too hard to understand you. You maybe know this about me, but sometimes I think about stuff too much. I have a hard time relaxing and trusting."

"Well, I think for today, you need to relax and," he paused, "you need to think about trusting me. Ready for a hike? How's your ankle?"

"It's good, I'm ready."

Chase called for Jake and led the way across the meadow. Today they were going to hike up to Chase's lake. They followed a narrow faint trail that wound through the pine forest. The climb was steep enough to make conversation difficult. Each had plenty to consider from their earlier conversation. Katie would have been surprised at how closely her thoughts mirrored his.

Complicated was the word. Chase wasn't surprised by her admission of being aware of being too introspective. Her comment that she admired him explained why sometimes she seemed intimidated by him. Now he appreciated she was trying to get past that.

Complicated was the exact word Katie used to describe him, his relationships and why he lived isolated in this beautiful place. He was self-sufficient and independent. He had a strong work ethic. He didn't need the constant feedback of being with others to be secure.

In that way they were similar, but she needed to be around people. Not because she needed affirmation, but because she liked the interaction with others. She enjoyed chit-chat as much as a serious conversation. People were interesting to her. It was important to her to personally make a difference in someone's life. Chase made a difference in people's lives through his writing, but at a distance from the reader and their daily lives. Interesting, she thought.

They reached the lake shortly and Katie could see why he would come here. It was a very small lake, with boulders and dense forest pitched down all around the edges, except for where they came out of the trees. Here there was a little grassy area that sloped gently to the water's edge.

Chase showed her the windbreak he had built out of the rocks. It wasn't much but on a blustery day you would be protected from the elements. The sun was warm and bright. Chase brought out the light lunch he had packed and they ate making small talk. They both brought something to read, but the warmth of the sun soon had Katie sleeping. She was relaxed and at peace with herself and the day.

Chase watched her for a while, thinking about how she had turned his otherwise quiet, secure life upside down. He had been so surprised at how much he had missed her after she left last fall. Despite their clashes, he had gotten used to having her around and when she was gone, the place seemed so quiet. In fact, he himself packed up his belongings for the year and left within a few days of her departure.

He wanted to follow her, but he did not know any more than her name and that she was from a small town in Minnesota. He googled her name, but there were so many Katie Carlson's in Minnesota he didn't know where to begin. He puzzled for months over what to do, all the while busily trying to finish his book. Finally, he decided it was something that wasn't meant to be and he ruthlessly pushed it from his mind. He didn't return to the cabin this summer at his usual time, early June. He couldn't quite do that. When he felt ready a few weeks ago, he made the trip. And now here she was again.

He knew this was his last chance, but he also knew there were a number of hurdles and it wouldn't be easy. Time was short, but maybe he should look at this as a beginning, not an end. Maybe they could make plans.

Without another thought he leaned over and kissed her lightly. Her eyes fluttered open and she found herself looking into the brown eyes that had haunted her for a full year. She reached up and pulled him to her. What started out as a gentle, tender kiss full of promise quickly turned into something more.

When he broke the kiss and pushed up from her, she groaned. She slid her hands from his neck to his shoulders. In his dark eyes she saw the question. Her breath caught in her throat as random bits of reason ran up against unleashed emotion.

There was no question she wanted him. She savored the strength of him, the feel of his body so close to hers, the smell of him – wood smoke and fresh air – and the taste of him. When he kissed her, she knew – she knew – no one else could make her feel this way. Question was, or problem, really; she wanted him forever and if she had just now, would that be good enough?

He saw her hesitation. He understood the source of it.

He drew her close, angling his head for another taste. "It's okay," he whispered against her lips. Her eyes held his.

"I want more," she said.

"I know," he said, "but we have this."

The sun was still warm, but the shadows long when later, in silence, they scrambled on the rocks at the lake's edge. This time, they both knew, would remain with them forever, no matter what the future. They didn't want to diminish it by speaking.

Quietly, they watched the clouds chase across the surface of the lake. Katie felt a lump growing in her throat. At the same time, she felt an odd sense of peace. She knew too, as Chase did, that leaving was the right thing to do.

She looked over at him at the exact same time he looked at her. She could see the understanding in his eyes. There was sadness there, too. An emotion she had never seen in him before. He reached out and cupped her face in his hands. Katie reached up a covered them.

"I am going to miss you," he whispered.

"And I you," she replied softly as she slid her hands down as his arms closed around her, drawing her close.

They held each other. She could feel the lump swell in her throat and her eyes misted, but the tears did not pour forth. After a while they slid out of the hug, his brown eyes held an odd sense of resignation. She felt her heart break, but the tears held. He had just said good-bye.

He stood and reached out a hand to help her up. "We better get back down before dark. No sense in taking chances."

"Fine," was all she could say.

Chase whistled for Jake and he came bounding out of the woods and around the lake. He was wet and happy.

22

Chapter Twenty-Two

Whispers slipped through
like air,
their presence always there.
Sadness.
Gone by, time.
When I was but a child
I heard a voice speak:
peace.
And peace led through
the whispers
which now lie silent.
In the darkness, death lies around our feet.
Crisp fresh death
Blowing in the wind.
A child's laugh is felt in

the back of time.
And smiles begin to break
the quiet dawn of beginning.

It was a beautiful day in late November. The air was crisp and fresh. Leaves fell and blew around, dancing in their freedom. Katie was on her way from one of the classroom buildings to her office. School had been in session over two months. Next week was Thanksgiving. It never failed to amaze her how quickly time passed.

Chase had been sadly reluctant to bring her to the airport in Portland. It was a quiet trip. Neither one felt like talking. Each was thinking about how tomorrow they would be apart, how what was supposed to be a beginning felt like an ending.

At the airport, the strain was beginning to take its toll. Chase wanted to ask her to stay, but knew he couldn't. Not yet. They had a lot of commitments. They each had thought about making plans, but the topic never came up. And now they were at the airport. He had a lot of thinking to do, more than he had ever imagined and he was prepared to do it. But now he was worried about Katie. She was so quiet, so grim, so determined.

"Are you going to be okay?" He asked.

"Sure. I'll be fine." She lied.

"I want you to be okay."

"I will be. I'll be fine. I have my …" she started to say commitments, but caught herself. Her commitments were merely an excuse to leave when she wanted more than anything in the world to stay with this dark, complex and wonderful man. But she didn't say anything more. She couldn't anyway. She had felt him say good-bye the day before on the mountain. Her eyes were full of tears as her heart began to break and she hadn't even boarded the plane yet.

She was surprised then, when Chase asked her for her contact information. It hadn't come up before.

"Here." She quickly fished out a business card. On the back she had written her home telephone number and address.

"Do you have a cell phone?" He asked.

"No. Between home and the office most people can get a hold of me. Do you?"

"Yes," he said sheepishly, almost embarrassed. "I'm not in one place long enough to maintain a land line anymore. My office prefers me to have a cell phone, even though they know it won't work most of the time. I promised I'd check it along with emails when I go into town every couple of weeks. I'll check today after you leave."

She was surprised to hear he maintained an office, a detail, he probably didn't think was important. She assumed he was going to give her his contact info but when he didn't she asked him for it. Much to her dismay he said no.

"Why?" She heard herself ask.

"Because, I don't know where I'll be or what my schedule is. I don't want you to worry when I don't answer my phone, don't return your calls or reply to your emails. When I know more, I'll let you know."

At her shuttered and hurt look he asked, "Is there a problem?" He had been afraid of her response but he was firm in his desire to control their future. He didn't want to make promises he couldn't keep.

"It feels like you don't trust me. I thought…" her voice trailed off. She could feel her emotions pulling at the little shred of control she had left.

Chase closed the space between them, pulling her roughly to him and kissing her fears away. "I want you to trust me in this," he said softly. He eased back and captured her eyes in his. "Please trust me. It's important that you do."

Katie understood now. If she was going to fit in his ever-changing life, she had to trust him. "Okay," she said. "I will."

Time stood still then as they prepared to part. They were only aware of the beating of their hearts and the pain that was already forming. It was time to board.

"Aw Katie." He whispered his eyes full of pain.

"Chase." She reached up and kissed him, hugged him hard and fled to the plane without a backward glance.

And now it was November. It had been over two months since she had left Chase in Oregon. Two long, challenging months.

He called once, shortly after she had gotten home. She could still remember how good it was to hear his voice.

"Katie?"

"Chase. Hi. Where are you?" She asked.

"I'm on my way to New York. You remember that tour I'm supposed to do this fall?"

"Yea."

"Well, I'm in New York for a week or so to catch up on business and finalize my schedule. Then I'm off."

"For how long?"

"Six weeks or so, depending on how it goes."

"Oh."

"Katie?"

"Yea."

"How are you doing?"

"I'm fine. Things are going okay. They rearranged my schedule of classes like I wanted, so now I have more time to write."

"That's good, isn't it? You don't sound too happy."

"No, it's good. But it's an adjustment and it's been harder than I thought."

"Oh."

Silence stretched between them.

"Katie. I've got to go. I miss you."

"I miss you too."

"I'll call again."

"Okay."

"Goodbye."

"Bye."

But he hadn't called again. Two weeks later she got the letter. It was postmarked Boston. It was as short as the phone call, but it held much, much more.

Katie, I miss you so much. Much more than I'd ever imagined. I love you. I know that now. Wait for me. Don't run. Please. Always yours, Chase.

Of course, she would wait. Of course, she wouldn't run. Not ever again. But that had been nearly four weeks ago. She hadn't heard from him again and she was getting frustrated. She knew what his schedule was. She was able to down load it from his web site. He was all over the United States, at all the big Ivy League schools.

She stared at her computer screen. There were two emails. One was from Chase and one was from the Dean Adamson. The subject line was the same, *convocation on Friday.* Before reading them, she knew, Chase was coming to St. Peter for convocation tomorrow, and this was the first she was hearing about it.

She opened the email from the Dean. He wanted her to introduce Chase Harrington at the Friday student convocation, since she taught Contemporary Affairs and used his books in class. This was a last-minute addition to Harrington's schedule, he said. But thought it was a great opportunity for the college. Would she be willing to introduce him and would she spend the day with him afterward? There would be a Dean's lunch and so on.

She opened the email from Chase. "I'm in Minnesota," he wrote, "coming to St. Peter tomorrow for convocation at the college. I can't wait to see you. This is my last stop on the tour for a while. Let me know you will be there. Thanks. Love, Chase."

She knew what she had to do and she didn't like it. But

aside from saying no and not coming in to work, she didn't have any choice. She replied to the Dean that she would be honored and she replied to Chase that she would be there. Then she left her office and wandered down the hall to Stan's office. She needed to share her news with someone. His office was dark. He was gone for the day. It was time for her to go, too. She would call and talk to Maria when she got home. She would call John, too. But she wasn't going to let her parents know. They knew enough, but they also knew she had come home without any commitments and only Chase's request that she wait for him. They had quit asking about him weeks ago. She wasn't about to raise the issue with them again until she was sure of something, one way or the other.

As she drove home with the late afternoon sunshine fading fast, she considered her options. She was angry. She was tired of the emotional treadmill she had been on. This year should have been better. There had been a hint of promise from Chase. But the silence was deafening. And now he was going to show up on her doorstop without any notice after weeks of silence. What was she supposed to think?

That was the question she raised when she talked to Maria. Her response did nothing to reassure her, "He asked you to wait, right?"

"Yes."

"He asked you to trust him?"

"Yes."

"So that's what you need to do."

"But that was months ago," Katie protested. "And now he just shows up here. How would you feel?"

"Probably the same. But you have to trust him and trust your heart. If you don't, then you might as well get ready to move on. At this point you don't have anything to lose, do you?"

"No. You're right. I know inside you're right, but I'm still angry about it."

"That's okay. I didn't say you didn't have a right to be angry. Just look beyond that. Don't let anger ruin what you might have with Chase."

"Okay, thanks."

"Do you want me to come tomorrow? Provide moral support?"

"Can you? That would be so great."

"The boys have preschool, so I can and will. You'll be fine," Maria said. "Just be yourself."

"Thanks Maria, for talking, for everything. See you tomorrow." She hung up the phone as Misty came to her.

"I think we need to go for a short evening run," Katie said. The last gray light of day left her enough time to pound out a couple of short miles and clear her mind. She knew Maria was right. She just couldn't shake the anger. She had kept a short leash on her emotions for over two months and now they were exploding as she anticipated facing Chase again. She was angry with him for his silence. She was angry that he was going to show up on her doorstep with so little notice. They had made no plans, he had made no promises, but she still had had some expectations. And she had been very disappointed.

Her conversation with John didn't help in anyway. In fact, he made her angrier. She told him the situation and asked, "What am I supposed to think?"

He said, "What was Chase supposed to think when you showed up on his doorstep in August? He had no notice. And there you were, again. The only thing that is different now is that he is showing up here. At least you have some notice. Give yourself a break, give him a break. Be happy he is coming."

"I know I should be. I really should be happy to see him. I am. Its, just, that I'd almost given up waiting and I'm having hard time trusting him."

"You took a chance last August, remember. Remember why and give him a chance now. I love you, Katie. This may be your chance for the happiness you've dreamed about. Don't let it slip away because you're angry."

"Can you come tomorrow?"

"No. You need to do this. You went to Oregon by yourself. You can do this. Come home this weekend if you need to, but I hope you don't."

"Okay, John. Thanks for listening. Thanks for your advice. I love you. I'll let you know how it goes."

#

After a restless night, Katie took Misty on an early morning run. Usually exercise helped manage her stress, gave her a chance to let her mind roam freely and helped her to plan and organize her day. Today was an exception.

She had learned years ago to hide whatever nervousness she felt. But that didn't do much to loosen the knots in her stomach as she prepared for the day. She decided to wear her favorite teaching clothes, something she was comfortable wearing and something she knew she looked good in, jeans, t-shirt and a jacket. It was casual, but professional and if she dressed outside of her normal style, it would raise eyebrows, if not with her students, then with her colleagues. Stan knew what was going on, but no else did and that was just fine with her. While she had an active social life with her peers, her private life was very much her own.

As she approached the auditorium, she looked good. Her stomach was still a mess. She only barely swallowed a piece of toast for breakfast. But she looked good and she had worked out how she was going to handle the day. She was going to be professional, because she was a professional.

Students were beginning to file into the auditorium, but she paused outside the door to take a couple of deep breaths to steady herself. Then she went in. She looked around quickly. Stan and Maria were near the front, but no Chase or Dr. Adamson. She had arrived late, on purpose, but they weren't there yet either. She made her way to Stan and Maria.

"Hey, thanks for coming," she said.

"You look great," Maria said. "How are you doing?"

"I'm really, really nervous, but otherwise good."

"You don't look nervous," Stan told her. "This will be easy. You've done it before."

"I'm not nervous about speaking," Katie told him firmly. "I'm nervous about seeing Chase. Oh, there he is."

They all turned to look as Chase and Dr. Adamson made their way toward the front. He had shaved his beard and trimmed his hair, but it was still longer than current fashion. He wore blue jeans but had traded in his flannel shirt for a classic blue button down and a navy jacket. He looked good.

"Wow," said Maria, "He's amazing."

"Maria," Katie said sharply, "You're not helping."

"What's so amazing?" Stan asked, all innocence.

"I'll tell you in a minute," said Maria. "Good luck, Katie," she added quietly.

"Thanks." Katie turned away headed toward the stairs to the stage. She caught up with Chase and Dr. Adamson at the foot of the stairs.

"Hi Chase." Katie said. "It's good to see you again."

Dr. Adamson looked startled. "I didn't know you knew each other."

"Yes," said Chase. "We met a couple of years ago out in Oregon, actually. On one of Katherine's trips we got to know each other. It's nice to see you too, Katherine."

"Well, good," said Dr. Adamson. "I had asked Katherine to introduce you because she teaches Contemporary Affairs and utilizes at least one, or is it two, of your books each semester. It seemed like a good choice based on that, but now even more so."

Chase wasn't listening to him, he was watching Katie. She was mad. He could tell. He heard her sarcasm even if the Dean didn't. He had worked hard to get this on his schedule and to end his lecture schedule here. But she didn't know that. She probably didn't know that he had been in Minnesota for two days, doing book signings and radio interviews.

He had stayed with his old friend from law school Steve Jackson, who had just moved from St. Peter to Minneapolis. There he was momentarily taken aback to learn that Steve knew Katie too. He was amazed Steve hadn't figured out Chase was the reason she had broken things off with him. But then Steve always looked at things from Steve's perspective, rarely considering other points of view. And it was surprising he even mentioned Katie to Chase, but when Chase told him he was going to St. Peter on Friday to speak at the college, Steve couldn't let it pass.

He silently agreed with him when Steve described her as "the most amazing woman he had ever met." That she was really pretty and smart. "But," he added, "she is always analyzing everything. Thinking about everything, and trying to figure out stuff. She has a very hard time relaxing and a very hard time trusting others."

Now as Chase watched her, he agreed wholeheartedly with his friend's assessment. But that didn't change his determination. It only furthered his resolve. The revelation that Katie used his books in her class was no surprise either. Steve had explained that too. And in doing so, revealed to him that his strategy for being here was the correct one.

Dr. Adamson was speaking directly to him and Chase shifted his attention to the moment at hand. "I will open up with a welcome, some announcements and then introduce Katherine who will then introduce you. As we discussed you have about 30 minutes and can take a few questions at the end. Again, I cannot express how much we appreciate you being able to be here today. It really is an honor."

"You're welcome," Chase answered graciously. "I'm very happy to be here too. I've heard a lot about your college and your community so I am glad I have a chance to see things first hand."

23

Twenty-Three

Katie's eyes flashed before she could catch herself. She was no longer nervous, she was mad. She had prepared some notes to use for her introduction, but she crumpled them up in her hand.

They made their way up the stairs with no further conversation and Dr. Adamson gestured them to their places. Three chairs were arranged behind the podium. Katie took one on the end. Chase wisely left the middle chair open for Dr. Adamson. He could feel the emotions radiating off Katie so he chose to let her simmer. After this lecture there would be plenty of time to sort things out between them.

Katie took a deep breath and looked out over the audience. Maria caught her eye and smiled. She could only manage a slight rising of her eye brows in return. Then she heard Dr. Adamson say her name, and the next moment he turned to her to welcome her to the podium.

She took her spot and smoothed out her notes. She glanced at them briefly, while she organized her thoughts.

"We are very fortunate to have Chase Harrington with us this morning. I am glad to see so many of my students here taking advantage of this wonderful opportunity to hear directly Dr. Harrington's philosophy. His lecture today is an interesting surprise.

"He is a nationally recognized philosopher, lecturer and writer. His newest book, Contemporary Affairs, is only the latest work in a long line of books laying out for the American people the consequences of our choices and what they mean to future generations.

"I personally had the opportunity to meet Dr. Harrington a couple of years ago. What he writes is consistent with how he lives. He is a man of compassion, integrity and intelligence. Join me in welcoming Chase Harrington today."

Katie turned to Chase and extended her hand in welcome. She met his eyes and he saw the confusion and conflict they contained. He held her hand for a moment longer and pulled her to him in a light hug. "Thank you," he whispered in her ear before he let her go.

He shuffled his papers for a moment while the applause died down in the auditorium. "Thank you," he said, looking out over the audience. "For those of you who don't know it, my recent book, Contemporary Affairs, is dedicated to Ms. Carlson, " he glanced at Katie just long enough to see the surprise on her face. "K.C."

Kaycee. The dedication had bothered her so much. Now it

was explained. But she wasn't sure what it meant. The book had come out before she went to Oregon last summer. When she arrived there last summer, he had seemed pleased to see her. Then he pulled back and before she left she thought he had made a commitment to her, but then he wrote a cryptic note and disappeared. Now he was here. And he had just made some sort of declaration, but she wasn't exactly sure what he had declared.

She looked at him as he was speaking. She didn't hear what he said. Some of her anger evaporated, but she was still upset. She didn't like surprises and he had sprung two on her today. If she was honest, she was very glad to see him and couldn't deny the pleasure of learning of the dedication. But she had vowed to not get back on the emotional roller coaster and that was where he was pushing her. She was going to push back.

Then he was finished speaking and sitting down again. She looked over to him and he caught her eye. He had that familiar half smile that stretched to his eyes, and there was more, there, a secret message she wasn't sure she wanted to know.

Katie heard Dr. Adamson dismissing the students and she and Chase stood. Dr. Adamson shook Chase's hand and thanked him again for being there. Thankfully, the Dr. did not mention the dedication. He turned to Katie, all smiles and pleased with the morning. "You are joining us for lunch in the President's room?" He asked her as they made their way off the stage.

This part of the day's events was not a surprise to her, but she was a little unsure how the rest of the day would unfold so she said she would be pleased to.

"Good." He said, "Especially since you already know Dr. Harrington. That will be a great help at lunch." He noticed Stan and Maria waiting at the doorway. "I invited Stan and his wife to join us as well as the rest of the history and philosophy departments. It should be a good group." He turned to Chase again, almost apologetically, "I hope this is alright with you. It is not every day we get a national lecturer here to our humble college. It is something I've wanted to do for years. Perhaps this will help draw others."

"Certainly," Chase said. "This is the last stop of my tour and after this I am going to be pursuing some personal interests. So I don't have any place in particular I need to be this afternoon and would be delighted to join your teaching staff for lunch and probably a discussion."

Katie listened to the exchange, dragging a little behind the two of them as they made their way down the aisle. Another interesting revelation dropped dramatically. She was the only one who understood what he was saying. After this afternoon, he didn't have any pressing commitments or obligations to attend to. She wasn't sure quite what to think.

When they got to the door, Chase let Dr. Adamson go on ahead and Stan and Maria went with him, leaving Katie to follow with him. As she drew near, she could feel her pulse quicken and her stomach turn. It only furthered her resolve to maintain some distance.

"That was a great lecture," she told him professionally.

"How would you know?" He answered, "You weren't even listening."

"That's not fair."

You're right, sorry. But thanks anyway." The smile that melted her heart months ago appeared. "So, help me out. How big is this lunch group going to be and how long will it last?"

She thought for a moment and appreciated the fact that he hadn't pushed the subject. "Probably around 20-25, more or less. Depending on if other spouses attend. Stan and Maria are friends of mine, but don't know what the others are doing." She answered. "These things are very informal. We are a small school, in a small town. But we've got good people here who are here because this is where they want to be. It is a lifestyle choice as well as a professional choice to teach at a college like this one."

He heard the pride in her voice and the assertion that this was where she wanted to be. They had never really talked about any of this anyway, so it shouldn't come as any surprise to him.

Dr. Adamson, Stan and Maria were long gone.

"Oops," Katie said. "We're behind. Let's go."

They made it to the Minnesota River Room in the Student Center and found everyone waiting for them. Stan and Maria were just inside the doorway and Katie introduced Chase to them first. Everyone said how pleased they were to meet each other. Katie watched him charm them and everyone else throughout the lunch. It did nothing to quell her anger.

Finally, it was over. Maria and Katie left Chase and Stan in deep conversation, making their way into the lobby area of the Student Center. The lunch was a huge success, breaking up only when professors had to leave for their classrooms. Katie could tell Maria was ready to burst. She was feeling the same way, only for a different reason. They reached the now quiet lounge area, Katie turned to her friend. "Well?" She asked.

"Katie, I can now understand the attraction. He is amazing. I can't believe he dedicated his new book to you. That must mean something. And he is here, too, with no immediate plans. What do you think?"

"If I wasn't sitting up front when he said he dedicated the book to me, I would have left. As it was it was all I could do not to roll my eyes or make a face."

Chase came up behind her at that precise moment. "Why?" he asked.

Katie slowly turned around and Maria quietly left. They were alone. Katie felt her annoyance and anger return.

"You tell me to trust you. You tell me to wait. And then you show up here with twenty-four hours' notice and then I have to introduce you and then you tell everyone you dedicated that book to me."

"I thought you knew. I thought that was why you came to Oregon this summer. I thought you figured it out."

"To Kaycee? How was I supposed to know?"

"I thought you were smart."

"I am. Just not smart enough for you." She started to leave. He grabbed her arm.

"You're angry."

"Really? What was your first clue?"

"Good."

"Good?" She looked at him for the first time, really looked at him. His dark eyes were warm and compassionate. He was waiting patiently for her to cool down. He almost smiled, she saw it in his eyes.

"You're laughing at me?" She pulled her arm away, but didn't leave. "Why are you laughing at me?"

When he didn't reply she thought for a moment, "This was a test, wasn't it, a test of my trust? How could you?"

"I had to. You've had me on a pedestal. I don't belong on a pedestal. Eventually I would have come down, but then what would happen? I had to push it along. I'm glad you're angry. You should be."

Katie was silent for a long time. He waited. Finally, she said, "What is going on here. Why did you come? Why didn't you call or email or anything? You just disappeared. I thought you had decided. How could you do that to me?"

"I'm sorry." He took a step closer to her. She held his gaze and took a step back. She didn't trust herself to be too close.

"Whether you realize it or not," he continued. "You know me almost better than anyone else. You know I don't need people. That bothers you and it scares you, I know. But I've learned I need you. I'm not happy alone anymore.

"That cabin in Oregon is the only place I call home. Everywhere else is some place I stay. And you know I'm only at that cabin a short time every year. I want a place to call home.

"This lecture series was something I had to get through. I was only marking time. I needed to get to the end of it so I could focus on my future, our future. I have the fortunate freedom to not be tied down, anywhere. I can do what I want from any place in the country, even here in St. Peter, Minnesota."

"What are you saying?"

"I'm saying I'd like to stay here. I'd like to be with you."

"Because? Why?"

"I love you. Okay?" He pushed his hand through his hair, his eyes flashing. "I'm tired of not being honest about it. I think I fell in love with you right away, the first time I saw you, but I denied it and let you go. You came back, but I've been on my own for so long I wasn't sure it could be different. Now I know. I love you and I'm tired of not being with you."

"That's a start. But I'm still upset with you. I need to go."

"Go?"

"Home."

"Okay," he suddenly wasn't as sure of himself as he thought he was. He knew she was mad, but he thought once he explained, told her why and that he loved her, everything would be fine. Frankly, he really never thought beyond getting here and seeing her and hoping her reaction would be what it was. But he didn't count on her pulling back. He thought it would be the other way around. "Wait a minute. You can't just walk away," he said. "After everything we have been through, you're just going to walk way?"

She kept her distance, but didn't move. Finally, she asked, "Would you like to see where I live?"

"Yes."

"Okay, would you like to have dinner with me? Say around 6:00? That will give me some time to get organized and for you to regroup."

She went to him then. "I am glad to see you, Chase. You are off the pedestal." She whispered in his ear before slipping out of his arms. "But you fell hard. And now, well, we need to regroup."

"I'm sorry, Katie," Chase said again. "I didn't mean to hurt you. I would love to have dinner with you. That would be a great start."

Katie pulled a notepad from her bag and wrote down directions to her house from the campus. She handed them to him, not trusting herself to speak. "Think you can find it?" was all she could say.

He looked at the paper in his hand, "Yes," he said, "I think so."

"Call me if you have trouble, otherwise, I'll see you tonight." She moved towards the door, needing space to get her emotions back in order. He nodded his response. He made no move to stop her, simply watched her nearly run out the door. He had time. He also had some things to do to make up for ground lost. If she wanted him to fight for her, then he would. It was his turn.

24

Twenty-Four

By the time Katie reached her home, she was pretty certain what she would do. The plan that began forming when Chase told her he loved her was becoming clearer. The remnants of her anger were dissipating but she could still feel those emotions fighting for control. Before she could do anything or make any decisions about the choices ahead she needed to clear her mind.

Five minutes later she and Misty were heading up towards the bluff line. As she took in the afternoon colors of autumn, she let her mind clear and just enjoyed the warmth of a late fall day. While the morning's run did nothing for her, this time she returned to the house relaxed and happy. Chase was here, in St. Peter, he told her he loved her and he was coming over for dinner. For the first time in weeks, she allowed herself to really hope.

It was already dark when Chase turned down the road to

Katie's house. He knew, though, she lived on the edge of town and that the views from her road included the broad scope of the river valley and that the November colors of brown on shades of brown provided a peaceful backdrop. He had ventured by soon after he had parted with her that afternoon. He wanted to make sure he knew how to get there before he took care of a few things.

The flowers that lay on the seat next to him took him nearly thirty minutes to pick out. He had wanted to do a dozen roses, but felt it assumed too much, but he wanted them to be beautiful and unique. He was glad he hadn't simply gone to Super-Value or Wal-Mart and picked out bouquet. He had had the florist personally design the arrangement and he felt it was perfect. Instead of a dozen roses, he chose a single red rose, surrounded by purple statice, white baby's breath and holly greens. It was early for Christmas, but he knew what he wanted this year.

He also went to the local coffee shop and purchased a bag of specialty beans. Finally, he had two bottles of wine, covering all his bases depending on what she was serving. She had, in fact, invited him to dinner.

He was prepared on all fronts. The fear of failure he had felt briefly in the afternoon was not something he wanted to feel again. They had been through a lot together and now it was time to be open and honest, to trust and be trusted. If they couldn't share the love, he knew they both felt, then they were both doomed for a life time of being alone, because, he knew, neither one may get another chance. He knew he wouldn't.

He pulled into her drive way and turned off the engine. Lights were shining from the windows, warm and welcoming. He heard a dog bark and then the back door opened and Katie stood waiting, the light forming around her leaving her face in the shadow. A dog pushed around her and came bounding towards the car.

Katie didn't move, as Chase opened the car door and got out. "Misty, come." She commanded. The dog obediently returned to Katie who absently petted her head all the while watching Chase reach back into the car for something. She saw the flowers in his hands and felt overwhelmed.

Silence stretched between them as he came up the walk. "Come in," was all she could say as she turned away from the door. Chase followed her into the sunny yellow kitchen. Katie was waiting. Her gray eyes were welcoming, but guarded. At the same time, the anger was gone. "   Hi." Chase said quietly, "these are for you." He put the flowers on the kitchen table next to him. Katie took a step forward, picked them up and breathed in their fragrance. She absorbed their unique beauty and understood.

She put them back down and reached for him. He moved to her. With their lips only inches apart, their breath commingling she barely got the words "thank you" out. He reached a hand behind her head, burying his fingers in her hair as he slowly brought his lips to hers. It was a kiss they would both long remember, for it sealed their fate. The flood of emotion Katie had been holding in overwhelmed her and she sagged against him. He easily held her and welcomed the relief he felt. It was all he could do to pull back, but he did, keeping her wrapped tightly in his arms.

He held her close, she savored the feel of him, the openness and love he shared. Eventually, they pulled apart, yet were reluctant to break the moment.

Misty, though, had no such reluctance. She nuzzled up against their legs, demanding to be noticed. They both laughed at once. "This must be Misty," Chase said as he bent down to pet her between the ears. Katie took advantage of the moment to regroup her thoughts and her plan. She wasn't sure anymore if she even needed her plan, but yet, there were certain things that needed to be taken care of.

There were a few last-minute things to do before dinner would be ready and after dinner she would show him around her house. He said he wanted a home. Well, this was it. She knew it and he knew it, but, she didn't follow the thought through. She had her plan.

"So," Chase said, "I take it you're not angry with me anymore."

"No," was all she said.

"Good." Despite the kiss, he knew he still had some ground to make up. His strategy may have been flawed, but he was here. He noticed the table set for two just through the open door. He picked up the flowers again from the table. "Where do you want these? On the table?" He asked as he started to move towards the dining room. She moved to take them from him.

"No. I have the perfect spot. I'll be back in a minute."

Misty still sat at his feet, looking at him with inquiring eyes. The smells of dinner wafting around reminded him of the other gifts he had left in his car. As soon as Katie came back, he said, "I've got a couple of other things in the car, I'll be back in a minute."

Katie looked at him blankly for a minute as he went out the door. When he came back with the wine and coffee, she went to him. He handed her the bag. She set it on the counter, and pulled out its contents. At her questioning look, he said, "I wasn't sure what we were having so I covered my options."

"We're having pork roast with apples, maple mashed sweet potatoes, salad and rolls."

"Okay," he came over and took one of the bottles from her. "You have an opener?"

She pulled one from a drawer, handed it to him and went to the cupboard for two wine glasses. As he poured, she pulled the salads from the refrigerator and took them to the dining room. She handed Chase the basket and bag of dinner rolls. "You want to put a few in this?" While he did that, she pulled the rest of the meal from the oven where it was warming. "All set. Dinner is ready."

She had deliberately set the tone to be normal and routine, even though this dinner and evening was everything but normal and routine. They had had plenty of high drama and emotion already that day, a little normalcy was in order. And it did feel normal, in many respects. That was also reassuring. As they took their places at the table, Katie took a moment to quietly observe Chase. He had replaced the blue button down with a dark green chambray shirt. His dark eyes were warm but intense as emotions danced through them. Katie felt herself getting lost in their depths. Chase raised his wine glass and Katie followed suit. "To us," he said simply. Not trusting herself to speak Katie reached out and touched her glass to his. So much for normal and routine, she thought.

They ate in silence for a few minutes, each struggling to find a safe topic of conversation. Katie's mind was nearly blank, her plan fading quickly.

"I really liked your college and town," Chase broke the silence. "The campus is beautiful and the town is small, but not too small. There seems to be plenty to do around here."

"Yes. I really like it here. Just for those reasons, and there are good people here. It's a good place to live." Realizing what she said and what he had said that afternoon helped her to return to reality. "Can you explain to me, again, when you decided to come here today and why you decided to stop communicating with me?"

Chase paused, put down his fork and used his napkin to wipe his mouth as he considered her question. He reached across the table and took her hand in his. His grip was firm and comforting. She tightened her fingers around his as dark eyes held gray.

"Look," he said. "There is one thing I want to be really clear on here. I love you." He paused for effect. "I may be made a mistake in my strategy to get here, but I am here now. That's the important thing. Not how."

"The thing is," she said slowly, pulling her hand back, "it feels like a dream to me. You being here, eating dinner with me. I'm afraid I will wake up and you will be gone again. I've been through so many levels of feeling today, it scares me."

"It wasn't an easy decision to be here. It was an easy decision to love you, but it wasn't an easy decision to be here. I've been on my own a long time. But you taught me there is more to life and to have more, I need to be with you. My work is important, but it didn't seem as important after I left you at the airport in Portland. It was really a long and hard fall." He stopped. "The important thing, here Katie, is that I am here and that I love you."

"Alright," she said. "But don't do that to me again. I don't like surprises and if you need help with strategy, check in with me first, because this strategy almost backfired." She smiled at him and the tension was gone.

When they finished dinner, Chase brewed coffee and helped Katie clean up. They moved comfortably around the kitchen together.

"Let's take our coffee in the living room." Katie took Chase by the hand but he had something else on his mind. He didn't move. Instead he pulled her back to him, took her coffee from her hand and pulled her into his arms. He captured her head in his hand, drew her to him, lightly touching his lips to hers. Katie sighed and slipped into the hug. She could hear his heart pounding or was it hers?

"Thank you for dinner," he whispered into her ear and turned her to kiss her again. This time it wasn't a light touch. She buried her hands in his hair and held on as her senses rolled. Chase pressed her even closer and then pulled back. "Too soon," he said.

She merely continued to grip his hand and turned to lead him through the house to the living room. They passed through the dining room and a closed door led to the porch that ran along the front of the house. She dropped his hand and went to turn on the gas fireplace that shared the wall with her study. Chase stayed where she left him, taking in his surroundings.

The room was all Katie. Along the back wall were floor to ceiling bookshelves nearly filled with books. A couch and a love seat were comfortably placed in front of the fire place and a small flat screened TV was in the corner. There were quilts, throws and pillows piled around the couch and love seat. Books were scattered alongside the sofa and it had an organized clutter to it.

"I didn't have time to really pick up too much in here," she said, a little embarrassed.

"I don't care," he replied. He saw the door by the fireplace.

She noticed and told him, "That is my studio."

He headed that way, "Do you mind?" He asked.

"No." She led the way and turned on the overhead light. She watched him closely as he stopped just inside.

It was a busy and colorful room. Painted yellow, like the kitchen, and there was fabric here and there. There was a big wooden executive desk set against the windows. He could see her lap top surrounded by notebooks and files. A printer was placed upon a low bookshelf. His flowers, as he liked to think of them, were placed on the desk next to a framed photograph. There was more floor to ceiling bookshelves, but they only held a few books. There were baskets and stacks of fabric.

He turned and saw a counter top, work area and a table with a sewing machine. On one wall was a large fabric covered corkboard and there were several designs pinned to it. This was something new and he liked it.

At his questioning look she said, "I like to sew quilts and work with fabric. I don't have a lot of time, so my projects seem to take forever. Usually, I do more in the summer, when I'm not in school. It's a nice break from teaching, reading and writing."

"This is something I didn't know about you. You never mentioned it."

"I don't talk about it a lot," she paused. "There are probably other things you don't know about me and there are probably things I don't know about you."

"True. Is that a problem?" He asked, not sure about her tone.

"I don't think so, unless you have a criminal record or a wife and children somewhere."

"Very funny."

They wandered back into the living room. Katie deliberately went to the sofa and sat down with her coffee.

Chase, however, went to the bookshelves. Katie waited quietly and watched him. He wanted to check something.

25

Twenty-Five

He stopped, stared and then reached out to run his finger along a row of books before turning to her. "You have all my books." He pulled one of his first books off the shelf and looked at it. Portions were underlined and notes were written in the margin. This book was well read. He put it back and looked at the others, same thing. She had told him about this, but now, seeing it, his thoughts trailed away and he once again remembered her startled look when he first introduced himself to her all those many months ago. This would explain why.

He went and sat down next to her, still holding one of his books. "This explains a lot of things," he said.

"Yes, I know. Here this will maybe explain some more or maybe not."

She handed him a copy of her most recent book of poems,

Traces, written in her pen name, Elizabeth Appleton. He looked at it, then back to her.

"You knew? Didn't you? That I had read your other book? That it meant a lot to me? I know you looked at all my books at the cabin. It wouldn't have been difficult to find. Interesting," he said.

"Yes," she said. "I knew. When I found it, it overwhelmed me and terrified me. It was too much too fast. And you seemed to be unaffected by everything while I was overwhelmed. On one hand I wanted to leave on the other I didn't. You were so remote. You took care of me, but you kept your distance. Yet sometimes I thought there was something more, but I was very confused by the whole situation and so when the time came to leave. I left."

"Tell me why you came back. Again, in more detail," Chase asked. His eyes were dark and questioning.

"Well," she said, "you're not going to believe it." She looked at him. "Are you sure you want to hear this?"

"Yes," he said. "I want to hear it, please. It is important to me."

"Okay." She paused as she gathered her thoughts. "Last July, I flew to New York to meet with my publishers and see if I could sign a multi-book contract, for more stability, and stuff, you know."

He nodded in understanding.

"While I was in New York, your new book came out and," she looked away, "of course, I bought it, right before I came home. Anyway, on the plane I took it out to start reading it.

But in looking at it, I thought there was something missing in your picture. That you looked different, sad, lonely, I don't know. And I thought," she stopped, embarrassed now.

"That was an old photo."

"Really? Well," she shrugged, "My imagination was working overtime, I guess."

"Go on."

"This part is really weird, and I am embarrassed to tell you."

"I know, but it's okay. Tell me. It doesn't matter."

"Well," she continued, relaxing a bit. "While I was looking at the book, my seat mate decided to start chatting with me. He said he had met you," at his look, she added, "you don't know him, I'm sure. He said he had been at a dinner party you were at last winter and just unloaded to me his opinion about you. As much as I didn't want to listen to him, I couldn't help myself. I was curious."

"What did he say?"

"Oh," she waved her hand, "just dumb stuff, like how he thought you had an attitude because he didn't think you had dressed appropriately for the event. That you were aloof and distant and implied you were rude. He also said he thought something was bothering you, and then shared rumors from earlier in your life. I pretty much stopped listening to him by that time, but it did make me wonder," she paused again, looking down. He reached over and took her hand. She looked back up at him. He smiled encouragingly. What did she have to lose, she thought. She might as well finish.

"I wondered if you felt the same way about me that I

felt about you. That maybe I meant more to you than you realized. I had been so confused and uncertain all year. And here was another reminder. I felt an overwhelming need to come back to you and see if what I felt was real and if you felt that way too.

"I needed to do it. I had questioned my feelings for you for so long and fought against them as being irrational that I decided I needed to find out or I would never have any peace."

She clutched his hand tightly, her eyes misting up. "So, I came," she whispered, "back to you."

Chase pulled her to him. The loop was finally closed. They were together, where they were meant to be. The relief was overwhelming. Katie lost herself in the strength and comfort of his embrace. Her plan was history. His strategy was flawed but worked. They finally realized that being in control wasn't nearly as important and that being honest wasn't as nearly as hard as they had thought.

Finally, Katie pulled away from him. She needed some physical distance. He didn't object, merely kept her hand in his. She had told him why she had come back. He had told her earlier, but now she wanted to hear it again.

"Tell me again," she said quietly, "Why you came here today."

He grabbed both of her hands in his. Dark eyes held gray and Katie held her breath as she waited. "Because I love you and want to be with you. That's it. There was no other reason for me to be here today, except for you."

He pulled on her hands and she was back in his arms. He kissed her gently before settling her against him. They sat and watched the flickering flames in the fireplace, each savoring how far they had come that day.

Then she asked the question that was foremost in her mind, "What's next for us?"

"We could talk all night about what's next. But you invited me for dinner, not for the night. Its late," he sighed. "I should go."

"I don't want you to." She reached for him and he held her close, close to his heart, where she belonged.

"Katie," he said quietly, "After a long time of writing our own stories, our own way, we both just got on the same page tonight. I'd like to explore the next chapter with you, but not write it tonight."

She leaned back in his arms, her hand resting on his chest. "What you are saying makes a lot of sense. But let me ask, because I have to, what is the time frame here? When do you have to leave?"

He covered her hand with his, "You didn't hear me this afternoon, did you."

She had, but she wanted to know what he meant. She shook her head no.

"My schedule is clear. Today was the last lecture in the series. I don't have a plane ticket to anywhere and my rental car is open ended. There are only two things. I would like to see Jake and I would like to take you home to New York for Christmas." He stood, pulling her up with him. "We have time."

He held her hand as he led the way back through the house to the kitchen door. Katie was no longer confused, she just knew that when he walked out the door, her house would feel empty again and she didn't like it.

Holding tight to his hand as he moved to open the door, "Just one more thing," she said.

He turned back to her.

"You said you wanted a home."

He studied her for a moment, his face in shadows by the kitchen door.

"Yes," he said. "There is a third thing I want. If I asked, would you say yes?"

She didn't answer, just shrugged her shoulders all the while her heart was pounding.

He said, "Is there someone I should ask before I ask you to marry me?"

She wanted to say no, but her father's face flashed before her. She knew it would mean a lot to him especially after all she had been though.

"My father," she said.

"That is what I will do then," he said, "before I ask you."

He held her briefly once more, and then slipped quietly out the door.

#

Over the course of the next week, they set their plans in motion as they continued to explore their future together. Chase would talk to her father when they gathered for Thanksgiving the next weekend.

Katie's parents were more than delighted to include Chase in their Thanksgiving meal. Katie and Chase drove down the night before so Katie could help her mother on Thanksgiving morning. Misty rode with them, lying quietly in the back seat. Chase was glad Katie had a dog, but he still missed Jake. It had been weeks since he had seen him. Normally, Chase didn't leave him this long, but this fall's schedule had been exceptionally tight and he knew Jake was in a good place, with his sister and her family at their orchard in upstate New York. Soon, if everything went according to plan, Jake would be in Minnesota too.

If Chase felt awkward by the greeting he received from Martha and Alex upon their arrival, he had the good grace not to show it. Katie had warned him. She knew how much they had both secretly longed for her to "find someone and settle down," as they put it. Thankfully, for the most part they kept those sentiments to themselves, but now meeting Chase, it was hard to hold back their feelings.

Martha had long known Katie's feelings, but had kept her thoughts to herself. Alex was caught completely by surprise by the turn of events. They were both looking forward to spending time with Chase.

"We're so glad you could join us for Thanksgiving," Martha said. "It's just our family, so it will be a quiet meal, but that way we can all visit a little bit more and just enjoy being together. John will be here tomorrow morning."

"It's nice to meet you, Chase," Alex said quietly. "I have to say we were a little surprised when Katie said she was bringing you," he stopped; the silence a little awkward, then he plunged ahead. "I'm looking forward to hearing your story."

"It's a long story," Chase said, wrapping his arm around Katie. "Katie will have to tell you about it when we have a chance."

"I think I know most of it. I'll tell it to you later," Martha said to Alex. "Let's take your stuff inside and get settled. Then we can relax or watch TV, whatever you'd like to do."

The evening passed quietly without having to tell the story of how they came to be together. It was a good story, but Katie was grateful they didn't have to share it right away. Their being together was still very new and she wanted to keep their story to herself a little while longer.

Thanksgiving morning, Chase and Katie agreed to split up. Katie wanted to spend time with her mother helping in the kitchen and Chase needed to spend time alone with Alex.

"Can I help you with your morning chores," he asked.

"I would like that," Alex answered. "I would also like to show you around our farm."

By then Alex knew the major parts of the story, but he didn't know much about Chase. Or exactly how they came to be together. Martha didn't either, and she was looking forward to some time alone with Katie.

"There was only once," she told him, "when she asked me what do to and I didn't have much advice for her. Since then she has kept all this to herself. I am so glad, though, that it seems to have all worked out. Don't you do anything to ruin it."

Martha's warning rang in his ears as he and Chase went outside. Alex decided to not push Chase on any subject, he just wanted a chance to observe. First, they fed the animals and Chase got a feel for the daily routine. They talked about farming and farm life and Alex found Chase understood the challenges of trying to keep a small farm profitable in an era where being big was all that really mattered. Alex liked him immensely for that and so, later, when they were returning from the driving tour of the fields Alex was ready to answer Chase's quiet question.

"I don't know you very well at all," Alex replied, "but I know my daughter. Her happiness is the most important thing to me. She's my only daughter and I love her very much. I don't have any concerns about her financial security. She's smart with money and from what I know about you, that isn't an issue either. But I am a little old-fashioned. I don't believe in divorce, if you get married, I expect you to work through the hard times, and I know there will be...I do know my daughter too!" He gave a chuckle and Chase smiled in response. He knew there was more.

"I can tell you love Katie and I know she loves you too. I would tell you that if you hurt her you'd answer to me. But Katie's her own person so all I can say is, I expect you to treat her with all the love and respect she deserves."

"That won't be a problem, sir."

"Then you have my blessing to marry her."

"Thank you, this means a lot to both Katie and I."

"You're welcome, thank you for asking me, you didn't have to. I appreciate it." Alex reached a hand out across the cab of the truck and Chase shook it.

"So, how soon are you planning on getting married" Alex asked casually as they made their way back to the house.

"Two weeks." Chase answered with a smile.

#

And they did. It was a small wedding, family and closest friends. Jake was there, brought by Chase's sister and her family. The photographer was very gracious in working the two dogs into the wedding pictures and all commented on how well behaved the pair were. It may have been a bit unusual, but then so was a two-week engagement.

Chase's parents were also there. They had never imagined this day would ever come and so they were content to enjoy it and looked forward to getting to know Katie when she came home with Chase at Christmas.

Katie was able to find the perfect dress off the rack in a boutique in Minneapolis. It was creamy white taffeta, with a scoop neckline. The bodice was plain, and the skirt swept around her in soft swirl. Chase gave her the delicate pearl and diamond necklace and earrings as a wedding gift. She wore her hair in an elegant upsweep with a pearl studded headband. She didn't want a veil to diminish her view.

The church was decorated for Christmas and so they just added a few personal touches. The flowers were evergreens mixed with red roses, sprigs of holly and baby's breath. Katie's bouquet was a simple single red rose, surrounded by white and pink roses, purple statice, white baby's breath and holly greens.

Chase's brother-in-law and Katie's brother, John, stood with him. Maria and Chase's sister attended Katie. Stan and Maria's little boys went down the aisle before the wedding party flinging rose petals.

Chase wore a black tux. In Katie's mind, as she walked with her father, he had never looked more handsome. From that moment on, Chase and Katie only had eyes for each other. They were lost in the warmth and sureness that their love would last forever.

The simple ceremony passed in a dream and suddenly, it seemed, the minister suggested he kiss the bride. For a moment, they stood there, with their fingers interlocked, unbelieving they were finally married. Chase's brother-in-law gave him a push and the moment was broken as Chase gathered Katie in his arms. The kiss they shared felt very familiar; full of gentleness, promises and hopes.

The ceremony and dinner were long over when they drove through the quiet streets of St. Peter later that evening. The stars were bright in the winter sky and if you looked hard enough you could see the northern lights flickering on the horizon. But neither Chase nor Katie were paying attention.

They were coming home, their home, together, at last.

Made in the USA
Middletown, DE
23 April 2022

64680481R00166